A Place Like Home

ALSO BY ROSAMUNDE PILCHER

Rosamunde
Pilcher

A Place
Like
Home

ST. MARTIN'S PRESS
NEW YORK

First published in the United States by St. Martin's Press, an imprint of St. Martin's Publishing Group

A PLACE LIKE HOME. Copyright © 2021 by The Literary Estate of Rosamunde Pilcher. All rights reserved. Printed in the United States of America. For information, address St. Martin's Publishing Group, 120 Broadway, New York, NY 10271.

www.stmartins.com

Library of Congress Cataloging-in-Publication Data

Names: Pilcher, Rosamunde, author.
Title: A place like home / Rosamunde Pilcher.
Description: First U.S. edition. | New York : St. Martin's Press, 2021.
Identifiers: LCCN 2021006925 | ISBN 9781250274953 (hardcover) | ISBN 9781250274960 (ebook)
Subjects: LCGFT: Short stories.
Classification: LCC PR6066.I38 P47 2021 | DDC 823/.914—dc23
LC record available at https://lccn.loc.gov/2021006925

Our books may be purchased in bulk for promotional, educational, or business use. Please contact your local bookseller or the Macmillan Corporate and Premium Sales Department at 1-800-221-7945, extension 5442, or by email at MacmillanSpecialMarkets@macmillan.com.

Originally published in Great Britain by Hodder & Stoughton, an Hachette UK company

First U.S. Edition: 2021

10 9 8 7 6 5 4 3 2 1

For Felicity

Contents

Introduction
By Lucinda Riley

When I was asked by Kate Howard at Hodder & Stoughton to write an introduction to a book of short stories by Rosamunde Pilcher, I felt immediately emotional. It took me back to a moment in my late teens when, like so many women in the UK and the wider world, I read *The Shell Seekers*.

It was a ground-breaking novel, in that it elevated the usual romance books we all read then to a deeper and more realistic level, introducing us to a not-so-perfect heroine and her often troubled family. It focuses on an older woman, no longer in the full bloom of beauty and youth, who reflects back on her life, with Pilcher's trademark vivid descriptions of her beloved Cornwall, where she grew up. Yet this was not a 'literary' book, but hugely accessible to all who turned its pages eagerly to discover what would happen. It was a wonderful *story* that was equally beautifully written, with memorable characters I can still remember to this day. In short, *The Shell Seekers* helped pave the way for many of us female novelists to write books that included 'romance', but gave a far more gritty and accurate portrayal of women living in the late twentieth century. As a young, aspiring writer myself, Rosamunde Pilcher and *The Shell Seekers* became my inspiration.

Like me, Rosamunde did not become an overnight success. She sold her first short story at nineteen whilst she was in the WRNS during the war, and in 1949 she published her first novel with Mills & Boon under 'Jane Fraser', a pseudonym she kept for ten novels before she began using her own name on all her books in 1965. It would take her another twenty years and twenty-two novels before she achieved worldwide fame with *The Shell Seekers* at the age of almost sixty.

Outside writing, Rosamunde had a long and happy marriage which produced four children. As her son Robin told me, in an era when it was still acceptable that children were 'seen and not heard', she always had time for hers. Many of Robin's friends who came to play would say that they wished she was *their* mother which, as a working mother of four myself, is perhaps the ultimate compliment.

Over the years, Rosamunde also wrote a number of short stories for women's magazines, some of which have already been published in collections such as *The Blue Bedroom* and *Flowers in the Rain*. After she sadly died in 2019, other short stories that had never been collated or published in book form were discovered at the British Library by Aoife Inman, an intrepid young assistant at the Felicity Bryan Associates literary agency, who spent days searching through old folios of magazines for stories Rosamunde had written, most of them between 1976 and 1984. Some of these are included in this new edition.

As with every Rosamunde Pilcher story – long or short – I

began to read them and couldn't stop. And as always, it took no more than a few pages before I came across one of her prosaic sentences: 'Loving a person . . . is not finding perfection, but forgiving faults.' Rosamunde had the unique gift of being able to sum up the essence of some of life's big questions in just a few wise words.

To those of you who already know and love Rosamunde's writing, these short stories will be a welcome pleasure, and for those readers that don't, they are a wonderful introduction to her talent as a storyteller and the fictional worlds she so effortlessly brought to life. Just as some of our most famous female novelists, such as Austen and the Brontë sisters, have stood the test of time, I believe that Rosamunde Pilcher's stories, all written in the twentieth century, will do the same – simply because she wrote so eloquently about universal themes that resonate with all women, whatever age they may live in.

Lucinda Riley
September 2020

A Place Like Home

Someone to Trust

When it was all over, when she had turned her back on him and walked away, leaving him standing on the pavement, staring after her, she had gone back to the office, stumbled through an afternoon's work, somehow got herself back to the flat, and then rung Sally.

The numbers slotted into place at last. She heard the double ring of Sally's telephone, far away in the uttermost reaches of Devon. She prayed, *Let her be in, please let her be in.*

'Hello!' Sally's voice, marvellously close and clear. All at once Rachael felt better. She smiled, as though Sally could see her face, hoping that the smile would somehow get through to her voice.

'Sally, it's me, Rachael.'

'Darling! How are you?'

'I'm fine. How about you?'

'Fairly desolate. Andrew's gone off for an unspecified period in his submarine. Probably crawling along under some terrifying ice cap or other.'

'Would you like a little company?'

'Adore it, if it was yours.'

'I thought maybe a couple of weeks?'

'I can't believe it! You mean, you can really get away from London for a couple of weeks? What about the job?'

'I'm tired of jobs. I'm giving in my notice tomorrow. Anyway, it was only on a sort of temporary basis. And there's

1

another girl who can take my room in the flat for the time being.'

'Oh, you couldn't have told me anything I wanted to hear more. When will you be here?'

'Next Friday week, if that's not too soon.'

'I'll meet you off the train. Darling . . .' Sally hesitated. 'It's frightfully boring. I mean, nothing but me and scenery, and I'm at the shop all day.'

'That's just what I need.'

There was another little pause, and then Sally said, 'Nothing wrong?'

'No, nothing.' But Sally would have to know, sooner or later. 'Well – everything, really. I'll tell you when I come.'

'You do that,' said Sally. 'Meantime, take care of yourself.'

Ten long days later and she was there. The train eased into the dark little station, the platform slid alongside. She saw the floodlit sign, Duncoombe Halt; a porter with a flag, a crate of chickens on a barrow. She stood up and heaved her suitcase off the rack and made her way to the door. She stepped down on to the platform, and saw Sally coming towards her. She put down the suitcase and was embraced in an enormous hug, and all at once nothing seemed quite so bad.

'Oh, how lovely to see you. Did you have a horrible journey, or was it not too bad?' Sally wore jeans and a raincoat and an enveloping woollen hat that came down to her eyebrows. She smelled of rain and open air and her cheek felt cool against

Rachael's own. 'Come on, let's go.' She had never been one to waste time with formalities. She picked up the suitcase and led the way, down the platform and over the bridge and out into the station yard to where her old estate car waited. The mist was drenching.

'It's rained all day,' Sally told her as they got into the car and she turned the ignition key. The windscreen wipers danced to and fro, headlights pierced the drizzling dark. 'Never stopped for an instant.'

'It's rained in London too.'

It seemed to have been raining ever since she had said goodbye to Randall. But it was different from country rain. Just as being miserable and alone in London was a world away from being miserable and with Sally in Devon. They left the station and came through the little town and were in the country in a matter of minutes.

'It's been a horrible winter, so cold and wet. There's scarcely a primrose showing and not a bulb in the garden . . .'

Rachael looked at Sally; saw the alert and childish profile that never seemed to change, the square chin, the slender neck. She was Rachael's first cousin, ten years older but closer than any sister. When Sally married Andrew, a lieutenant-commander in the Navy, Rachael had been her bridesmaid; and when Rachael grew up and went to live and work in London, Sally was all enthusiasm, because now, she said, she had a cast iron excuse to come to town, to have lunch with Rachael and trail around the Tate Gallery while Andrew was attending some nameless conference at the Ministry of Defence.

It was Sally's and Andrew's reaction to Randall Clewe, politely enthusiastic, but unmistakably wary, which had first caused Rachael to stand back, as it were, and take her first, cool appraisal of him, forcing herself to see him through Sally's eyes. After that she became aware of his imperfections, but she was still in love with him. Loving a person, she had told herself, is not finding perfection, but forgiving faults. She went on telling herself this for nearly three years.

When she had first met him, Randall had been married, with two children; he was now separated from his wife.

'You don't want to get involved with a married man,' Sally had said. 'You'll get hurt. It's all too complicated.'

'But it's happening all the time,' Rachael had protested.

'Not to people like you. You're too vulnerable. You'll get hurt.'

'I can't get hurt if I know the situation.'

'But do you know the situation?'

'He's trying to get a divorce.'

'But the children! And what's going to happen to his wife?'

'They haven't been happy for ages. He has to be away so much. His job takes him abroad all the time, and she's resentful . . .'

'More likely lonely . . .'

'Anyway, he sees his children.'

'If he gets a divorce, is he going to marry you?'

'We haven't talked about it.'

'I think you're wasting your life.'

'It's my life.'

'It's too good to waste.'

'As I said, it's my life.'

It was the nearest they had ever come to quarrelling. At the end of the discussion, with neither of them giving an inch, they had not talked about Randall again, but simply carried on as though the argument had never taken place. Sometimes when Andrew and Sally were in London, they all went out for dinner together, always to an exorbitantly expensive restaurant of Randall's choice, and always with Randall insisting on picking up the bill. This rankled with Andrew. His tastes were modest to match his financial resources, but he had a natural masculine pride, and there was always a slight atmosphere at the end of the meal when Randall, his cigar lit and his brandy glass empty, slapped down his credit card with scarcely a glance at the heart-stopping sum scribbled at the foot of the bill, and suggested that they all go on to a night club.

Sitting in Sally's car, remembering all this, Rachael was suddenly visited by Randall's image. His good looks, the smell of his aftershave, the expression in his eyes as he watched her across some candlelit table. Her physical longing for his presence made her tremble. To and fro went the windscreen wipers. Never again, they said. Never again. Never again.

Sally was still talking, needing no comment to encourage her flow of chat.

'. . . it's marvellous having the shop because it keeps me busy while Andrew's away. You did know about the shop. I told you, didn't I, that I scraped all my resources together and bought it from the woman who used to run it? I helped her for a bit before she sold up, so I learned all about buying in stock and doing accounts, and it really hasn't been too much of a headache.'

Rachael pushed the image of Randall out of her mind, took a deep breath and said, 'It's a craft shop, isn't it?'

'Yes, right here in Duncoombe. There's not much trade in wintertime, but in the summer it goes like a bomb.'

'I'll have to come and see it.'

Ahead of them lay the lights of the little village of Tudleigh. Beyond Tudleigh loomed the dark bulk of the moor, and above the village a light shone through a copse of elms. This was Sally's cottage, which Andrew and Sally had bought five years before when Andrew was stationed in Plymouth. They came through the winding street of thatched houses, and then turned up the steep lane which led to the cottage itself. Elms arched overhead, the white gate stood open. The car bumped over the ruts, and there was the house, the light shining, as Sally had left it, over the front door.

She went to open it, fumbling in her pocket for the key while Rachael heaved her suitcase off the backseat. Inside was the little hallway, warm and smelling nostalgically of paraffin lamps. Sally shut the door behind them, turned on the lights and led the way up the wooden staircase and into her tiny guest room with its sprigged wallpaper and sloping ceilings.

'You'd like a hot bath. I know you'd like a hot bath better than anything else.' She drew the curtains. 'And then we'll have a drink and supper by the fire.' She turned from the window and, for perhaps the first time, really looked at Rachael. 'You're terribly thin. Have you been losing weight?'

'Not meaning to. But all my skirts and jeans are far too big.'

'I'll fatten you up,' said Sally firmly. 'Lots of Devonshire cream. Now make yourself at home, and I'll go down and peel the spuds.'

When she had gone, Rachel stood there, in the middle of the room in her travel-weary clothes, suddenly exhausted. She took a deep breath, and let it out in a long and shaky sigh. The break was behind her. She was here. Now, physically, she had truly withdrawn from Randall. After a little, she unbuttoned her coat. She hung it up and began to unpack.

A scalding bath, a change of clothes. Warm and refreshed, she went downstairs and found Sally in the sitting-room, by a roaring log fire, watching television. When Rachael appeared, she switched off the television, gave Rachael a smile, and together they went into the kitchen to get their supper. There was soup, and steak and kidney pie, and Sally opened a half-bottle of wine.

'I don't know what it's like. Andrew always buys the wine. But I get it from the off-licence in Duncoombe and the man assured me it was modest but full-blooded.' She pulled the cork with a triumphant yank, set the bottle on the tray and carried the whole lot through to the sitting-room where they settled themselves in armchairs on either side of the fire and proceeded to demolish the delicious meal.

———

It was not until they had cleared the dishes and were back by the fire with mugs of coffee that Sally broached the subject of Randall. She didn't do it in so many words, simply waited for a natural pause to break their conversation, and then said, in a changed and gentle voice, 'Do you want to talk now or would you rather wait?'

Rachael met her eyes. 'I don't know.'

'You said on the telephone that everything was wrong. It's Randall, isn't it?'

'Yes.'

'It's over?'

'Yes.'

Sally said, 'I'm sorry. I'm sorry because I know how much he meant to you. But I'm glad as well.'

'You never liked him. You or Andrew.'

'You couldn't help liking Randall. He could charm the birds off the trees. But we always felt he wasn't the right man for a person like you. He was too – too much of a good thing, I suppose. A fair-weather friend. And the fact that he was married . . .'

'He got a divorce,' said Rachael flatly.

Sally's eyes opened. 'He did? When?'

'About nine months ago.'

'You never told us.'

'I didn't tell you because I thought that as soon as you knew, you'd be expecting us to get married. I didn't want to have to tell you that nothing seemed to be any different. We just went on. Marking time. I didn't want Andrew saying, "What the hell's he playing at?"'

'And what the hell was he playing at?'

'He was . . .' Rachael folded her fingers around the warmth of her coffee cup and stared into the fire. 'He was free. He didn't want to be anything else. Free to come and go, take out any girl he wanted. Free to go to Hong Kong and enjoy himself, without any strings. Free to take his children away and no questions asked. Free . . . simply to be himself.'

'And you were still there.'

'Oh, yes, I was still there. In London. Handy when he wanted me. And yet he never made it feel that way. Every time we went out it seemed to be some sort of celebration. Every time he came back from somewhere, he was laden with presents, with love and every sort of enthusiasm. Just to be with Randall made me feel vital and beautiful. As though that was the way he always saw me.'

'But he didn't love you?'

'I suppose, in his way, he did. But Sally, three years is a long time. We'd done it all. Been on holidays together, to Gstaad to ski, to Monte Carlo for the weekend. But it was like playing games all the time. It wasn't living. I couldn't go on playing games, Sally.'

9

'Did you tell him you wanted to get married?'

'No. And by the end I wasn't sure that I did. But after the divorce he asked me to go and live with him – move into his flat. I very nearly did. I wanted to, but somewhere, right at the back of my mind, was this image of myself, one day, packing my suitcase and moving out again. Somehow it was the ultimate degradation. And I was frightened. So I clung to my pride and stayed on my own.'

'Thank heavens for that,' said Sally.

'Anyway, about a month ago, I began to realise that there wasn't any future in it. Not for Randall and not for me. And I decided that if it had to finish, then it had to be me who did the finishing because he never would. So, that day I rang you, we went out for lunch. And I spent the whole of that lunchtime trying to make him understand that I'd come to the end of the road. And he didn't understand and he still didn't believe me. We came out of the restaurant, and he started to tell me he was flying to Copenhagen, but he'd be back next week, and he'd ring me, and I said, "Goodbye, Randall." And he just stopped talking and stared at me as though I'd gone mad. And I said it again. And that time he didn't say anything. And I turned round and walked away from him. And I haven't seen him since.'

Sally said gently, 'It's like pulling up roots, isn't it? You feel as if you're going to wither up and die.'

'Yes. Half alive. Incoherent, incapable. Waiting for a telephone call which you pray will never come. Irrational.'

—◆—

A log crumbled and broke in the fireplace. Sally got up and fetched another and threw it on to the bed of glowing ashes. She said, 'It does pass, you know. Horrible old cliché about time healing.'

'I know. I keep telling myself.'

Sally perched once more on the edge of her chair, leaning forward, her expression eager. She said, 'You mustn't go back to London till you've got over this. You must stay here, for as long as you like. Andrew won't be back for at least a month, and even when he is back, he'll love having you here.'

'But . . .'

'If you don't mind being alone, because I have to be at the shop all day. But there's heaps you can do to help me or you can go for long restoring walks, or weed the garden. And it will soon be spring, and you'll feel different. Everything will be quite different when the spring comes. What do you think about it? What do you think about staying?'

The relief of not having to return to London was so great that Rachael felt her eyes fill with tears. She tried to laugh in order not to cry. To say, *oh, I'd love it*, but the words wouldn't come out and she cried anyway. It was the first time she had cried since the gruesome day she had left Randall forever, and once she started she couldn't stop. But there was only Sally to see, so it didn't matter.

It was lovely being alone. The weather was damp and calm, mild quiet days when sometimes a gleam of sunshine showed through the clouds; sometimes showers were blown in off the sea, leaving the winter earth dark and sweet-smelling. Rachael went for walks around the baffling Devonshire lanes. One day, she climbed up on to the moor and met a herd of wild ponies. She walked down to Tudleigh and did Sally's shopping in the little village store, and the local people said 'Good morning' and stopped to discuss the weather.

One morning she went with Sally to Duncoombe and had her hair done in the local beauty parlour. Afterwards, she walked down the high street to Sally's shop, in order to pick her cousin up and take her out for lunch. Sally was at her desk, doing sums, so Rachael wandered around the shop, inspecting the pottery, the pictures, the mohair shawls, the charming little accessories in gingham and print. 'What sort of a morning have you had?' she asked.

'A good one,' Sally told her. 'Business is picking up. By Easter we'll be going flat out. I think I should stand you lunch today.'

'That wasn't the arrangement.'

'We'll toss for it.'

But they never got around to tossing for it, because at that moment the door opened with a tinkle of the bell, and a man came into the shop. Rachael turned her back, pretending to be a browsing customer, and she heard Sally say, 'Good morning,' and then go on in a changed voice. 'William! What are you doing here?'

'Hello, Sally. I've come to do some shopping.'

A deep voice. A very attractive voice. Rachael picked up a

rag doll in a mob cap, with an embroidered face and bright blue eyes.

'What for?'

'A wedding present. One of the young assistants in the office is getting married, and I thought you might have something suitable. A casserole, perhaps, or a picture.'

'Yes, of course.' Sally stopped. 'You haven't met Rachael, have you?'

'No.'

Rachael turned to face them, still holding the doll.

'She's my cousin, she's staying with me. Rachael, this is William Clifford, an old friend of Andrew's.'

'Hello, Rachael,' said William Clifford. He was tanned, his thick hair silvered with early grey, his face was bony, his shadowed eyes grey. He wore a comfortable-looking tweed suit and a checked shirt. Perhaps a farmer, dressed for market day, or a country lawyer.

'Hello,' said Rachael.

'Are you helping in the shop?'

'No. Just waiting for Sally to come out to lunch with me.'

'Then I mustn't hold you back.'

'We're in no hurry.'

In the end they were all involved in his purchase and it was Rachael who found the pair of sporting prints.

'Those would make a really good present,' she told him.

Sally laughed. 'You're a real friend, Rachael, those are just about the most expensive things he could buy.'

But William Clifford agreed with Rachael, and said he

didn't mind about their being expensive, so Sally wrapped them for him while he wrote the cheque.

As he signed his name, he said, 'How long are you staying for?' He looked up at Rachael, and she realised he had been addressing her.

'For a little.'

'That's good.' He smiled towards her, handed over the cheque and picked up his parcel. 'I hope you enjoy your holiday.'

When he had gone, 'Who's that?' asked Rachael.

'Oh, he's a sweet man. We've known him for years. He's an architect in Plymouth.'

'Does he live in Plymouth?'

'He used to, but he's bought himself an old barn up at Farhampton on the edge of the moor, and he's converting it into a house.' She slammed the till shut and looked at her watch. 'Come on,' and she reached for her coat. 'I'm hungry. Let's go and buy ourselves a ploughman's at the Dog and Duck.

Three evenings later, as Rachael climbed out of her bath, the telephone rang downstairs. She heard Sally go to answer it, and Sally's voice. And then Sally coming upstairs.

'Rachael.' She opened the bathroom door. 'That's William Clifford on the telephone. He wants to talk to you.'

Rachael, wrapped in a towel, sat on the edge of the bath and looked dubiously at Sally.

'What does he want?'

'He said something about going up to Farhampton with the contractor. He wondered if you'd like to go, for the drive.'

'When?'

'Tomorrow morning.'

Rachael pulled the towel more closely about her. 'I don't want to go.'

Sally frowned. 'Oh, Rachael. Why not?'

'I just don't want to.'

'Look, you can't sit around moping forever. It's just a drive in the country.'

'I don't want to.'

'Well he's waiting on the end of the line. Go on.'

There was nothing for it but to go, as Sally was obviously not going to act as messenger. With her wet feet making marks on the floor, Rachael went downstairs to pick up the receiver.

'Hello.' *I can't come, I'm so sorry, I know you'll understand.*

'Rachael.' She had forgotten the warm depth of his voice. Suddenly, she saw him again. His bulk and size, the comfortable ambience of his presence. 'I don't know if Sally told you, but I'm going out to Farhampton tomorrow morning, and I thought if you weren't doing anything else you might enjoy seeing a bit of the country.'

'Well, I . . .'

'If I picked you up about half past ten, would that be all right?'

The excuses melted away. She had no excuse, anyway, no good one. 'Yes, I . . .'

'Great. Wear warm clothes. It's cold up on the moor.'

'All right.'

'I'll see you then.'

He rang off, obviously not a man for small talk. Slowly Rachael replaced the receiver. Sally watched her from the open door. She was smiling. Rachael said, 'Is he married?'

'Of course he's not married. He's our local eligible bachelor.'

'I said I'd go.'

'I heard.'

'I couldn't think of a single excuse not to go.'

'It was such a harmless suggestion that it was hardly worth bothering,' Sally said drily. She grinned again. 'Now you're back in circulation.' And with that, she went off, whistling, to the kitchen, to see about their supper.

———

That night a wind blew up and the next morning dawned bright and bitterly cold. There was frost on the land, and seagulls, blown inland by the storm, glided screaming over the ice-hard fields. Rachael put on corduroy trousers and an ancient sheepskin coat of Andrew's which she found in a cupboard, and a few minutes before half past ten the big car came bumping up the lane, stopped in front of the cottage, and William got out.

She went to meet him, locking the front door behind her. He said, 'I'm a little early.'

'It doesn't matter.'

He was bundled into a high-necked white pullover under a heavy coat with a wool collar, and he grinned cheerfully as he opened the door of the car for Rachael. 'There's a change in the weather.'

'I didn't think it could be so cold in Devon.'

'Now you know why the primroses haven't come out.'

The car was warm. They drove back down the lane, and through Tudleigh, and turned up on to the road which led to the moor. The land dropped beneath them, sparkling beneath the bright wintry sky. Soon, in the far distance, could be seen the straight, silvery line of the sea. They came through moorland, bracken-brown and dark with peat, and there were high tors of granite on the summits of the shallow hills, and sheep, and herds of wild ponies.

He talked, easily and naturally, telling her about the old barn at Farhampton, which he had found by chance, on his way back from a job north of Exeter. He said, 'I always wanted to live in the country, but it's hard to find a property that doesn't have acres of farmland, and I'm too busy a man to cope with that.'

They came up a hill and crested a rise and the moor lay ahead, like a sea, undulating to the horizon. Rachael said, 'It's so beautiful.'

'Where do you live?'

'In London, mostly.'

'I like London too.' She thought of all the things she loved about London. The sky at night, and the river, and coming out of a restaurant into the cold; taxis and the smell of flowers on barrows when you least expected it. And, inevitably, Randall. But this was no time to think of Randall. Rachael pushed his memory out of the way, out of sight, as though she were shutting him into a box, sitting on the lid. 'I like London a lot.'

They came at last to his property. It lay just beyond a small moor village, down a deep lane. Everything seemed to be muddy. She saw the bleak, roofless shape of the old barn. Stones and piles of brick lay around; planks of wood and concrete mixers, a battered iron wheelbarrow. A car was already parked in the midst of all this, and as they approached, the door opened and a man in a duffel coat emerged. 'The contractor,' said William.

They stopped beside him and got out of the car. William introduced Rachael, and then he and the contractor went off together, with plans and foot-rules, and Rachael was left to nose around by herself. She saw the view, and smelled the bitter cold of this high, upland air. She walked a little way, but the wind was icy, cutting through all her warm clothes and making her ears ache, so she went back to the gutted barn and found William saying goodbye to the contractor. Later, when he had gone, they returned to the empty shell of the building, the walls open to the sky, the floor beneath them a hopeless mess of rubble and mud.

'If it were me,' said Rachael, 'this is where I would throw in the sponge and go home. It all looks so desolate.'

He smiled, understanding. 'I've got over that stage. This is the worst. After this, it can only get better.'

'You're rebuilding.'

'That's right. Virtually rebuilding. You see, this will be the sitting-room. And there, the fireplace. And then a kitchen here. No upstairs, but a deep gallery, with two bedrooms and a bathroom. And then here . . .'

But she had stopped listening to his words, heard only his voice. She thought, there is something warm about him. He's not all that attractive. He's not even very young. But you know that if he said he'd do something, then he'd do it. He wouldn't ever let a person down.

———•—•———

'How did it go?' asked Sally.

'All right.'

'Did you see the house?'

'Yes.'

'Is it pretty?'

'It will be one day.'

'Did William give you lunch?'

'You're being cagey, aren't you?'

'There's nothing to be cagey about.'

'But do you like him?'

'Yes, I like him. That's all. Just like him.'

'Is he going to take you out again?'

'I shouldn't think so.'

She told herself, convinced herself, that the drive to Farhampton had been a one-off thing. That was the end of it. But two evenings later William, in passing, called in at the cottage for a drink, and to ask Sally and Rachael to a visiting ballet which was performing in Exeter.

It was *Coppélia*, and afterwards he took them out for a festive dinner. It transpired that he was a charming and easy host. As he talked to Sally, Rachael watched him covertly and wondered how he had looked as a very young man, if he had always possessed this tranquil and calm disposition. She found herself wondering why he had never married. Later, when they were home again, she asked Sally.

'Why has William never married?'

But Sally was vague. 'I don't know. I suppose he never met anybody he wanted to marry. Anyway, he's still quite young. Those grey hairs are misleading, I know, but he hasn't got one foot in the grave yet.'

Two mornings later, when Rachael was alone in the cottage, he telephoned again. The call came when she was in the throes of cleaning Sally's oven, and she had to go to pick up the receiver with an old towel wrapped around her dirty hand.

'Hello.'

'Rachael, it's William.'

'Good morning.'

'What are you doing with yourself?'

'Cleaning Sally's oven.'

'Would you come out for dinner tonight?'

She had been half-expecting this, and yet, now that the moment was upon her, panicked. She shied instinctively from the thought of some expensive restaurant, candlelight, and wine. She knew that she wasn't yet ready for such intimacy. It wasn't that she didn't like William. He was a disarmingly easy person to like, but she was frightened of their relationship moving further. Pleasant threesome evenings with Sally were well within her depth, but beyond that . . .

'I . . . don't think . . .' she began to say, but he interrupted her.

'It's some old friends of my parents. They've got people down from London for a race meeting at Taunton, and I've been invited for dinner. I said I could bring you, and was told "of course". I thought you might like to meet the Kinnertons and see their house. It's worth seeing.'

'Well . . .' A dinner party in another person's house could scarcely be counted as dangerously intimate.

'Sally wouldn't mind, would she?'

'No, of course not.'

'Then you'll come?'

'I'd like to.'

'Great. I'll pick you up about seven fifteen. Till then.'

———

Characteristically, he rang off before she could think of any more objections to his plan. Rachael was left standing, with the buzzing receiver in her hand. She replaced it, but did not go straight back to the kitchen. Standing by the empty fire-place, she looked up and met her own eyes in the mirror over the mantelpiece. *It's all right*, she told herself. *He's not like Randall. He won't hurt you, and if you have any sense you won't let yourself be boxed into a situation where you find yourself hurting him.*

'*Would you come out for dinner tonight?*' Forthright and uncomplicated. He wouldn't turn up, unannounced, out of the blue, only to leave her again, with no warning and no farewells. She thought of Randall, saying he would call, forgetting to call, and then sending flowers to fill the flat. She felt the pain again, the ache of longing, the trembling that was wanting him. She thought, *It isn't any better. It will never be better.* But standing looking at herself could do no good, so she went back to the oven and continued, doggedly, with her mindless task.

Sally said, 'The Kinnertons. Oh, you lucky girl. You'll have a wonderful time. They're aged and rather grand, and their house is filled with beautiful things.'

'You're giving me cold feet.'

'What are you going to wear?'

They went upstairs to find something. Sally produced her best evening skirt, Rachael a silk shirt, very simple, which seemed suitable for the occasion. A wide gold belt would cinch the two together. She washed her hair and was doing complicated things to her eyelashes when she heard his car come up the lane, the opening and shutting of doors, and Sally's voice as she let him in. When Rachael went downstairs, Sally was sitting by the fire, and William standing with a shoulder against the mantelpiece, his hands in his pockets, talking to her. He wore a dark velvet jacket and a bow tie and looked immensely distinguished, and as Rachael came through the door, he turned to smile at her.

'Don't you look good.'

'Thank you.'

He straightened up, glancing at his watch. 'We ought to go.'

As they drove, he told her about the Kinnertons. 'He and my father were in the Army together. I've known them all my life. Their son Ben was my friend. She's a manic gardener, and he's a JP and sits on the bench and drives everybody crazy because he seldom remembers to turn on his hearing aid.'

They came at last to the house, driving up through impressive gates and a winding, tree-lined driveway. The surface of the road was appalling, rabbits darted to and fro in the glare of the headlights, but when they turned the last curve of the drive, the house lay before them, and Rachael saw the long, low shape of an Elizabethan manor, random lights shining from the leaded windows. As they drew up, the front door was opened, and a pack of assorted dogs poured at them, barking senselessly, but without rancour. Behind them came their host. A tall, white-haired and white-moustached old gentleman, hawk-nosed and dignified. He wore a dinner jacket which was probably fifty years old and a prehistoric hearing aid wired to one ear, and attached to a bulky contraption which he had tucked in the top pocket of his jacket.

'Hello, my dear boy, splendid to see you.' He had a high hooting voice of a very deaf man. 'And who's this? Rachael, you say? How do you do, my dear. Now come along in . . .'

They followed him indoors and he shut the door. The hall was large and panelled and rather dusty. Dogs' baskets and drinking bowls stood about, along with some gardening boots. There were beautiful, faded Persian rugs. A sullen fire burned in an enormous grate, giving off no heat whatsoever, but they shed their coats and were led into the library, and here a much more cheerful fire burned behind a tall club fender, and there were sagging sofas, and more dogs, and cupboards filled with exquisite china, and a great many family snapshots in tarnished frames.

Mr Kinnerton was pouring their sherry when the door opened and they were joined by Mrs Kinnerton, as small and plump as her husband was tall and thin. She wore a black velvet dress, with one or two diamonds pinned haphazardly upon the bosom. Her hair was equally haphazard, bundled into a vague knot, and thus she bore down on them, smiling and cosy.

'Oh, William, so lovely to see you. Give me a kiss. So good of you to come at such short notice.' She raised her voice. 'Darling, are you pouring sherry, because I want a whisky and soda.' She turned to Rachael. 'I can't tell you what a day I've had. These friends of Ben's asked if they could stay for the Taunton races tomorrow, and I completely forgot it was my cooking lady's weekend off. So I've been struggling in the kitchen.'

'How many people have you got staying?'

'Only four. But it seems to mean an awful lot of potatoes to peel.' Her hands were a gardener's hands, knotted and rough, the nails broken. She was not the sort of woman ever to wear rubber gloves.

'It was sweet of you to invite us, too.'

'Well, you know, these young people, they don't want to spend an evening with boring old us. That's lovely, darling!' She shouted at her husband as he gave her her drink.

He said, mildly, 'You don't have to shout. My contraption's turned on.'

'I never know when it is and when it isn't.' She laughed gaily, and Rachael laughed too, because somehow with Mrs Kinnerton even the hearing aid had turned into a joke. 'Now, come and sit by the fire and tell me what you're doing in Devon . . .'

But there was no time for this because at that moment came voices and footsteps from the direction of the hall. The door opened and four people came in. Two men and two girls. One of the girls was slender in red culottes; the other in flame-coloured chiffon. One of the men was tall and fair. The other . . .

———•◦•———

Standing close to the roaring fire, Rachael felt herself grow icy cold. She heard the steady thud of her own heart, and a shivering tremble passed, like a shock, through her body.

'Now, I must introduce you all. Charles and Miranda Bailey, and this is Lucinda Bailey, and Randall Clewe.'

Rachael's fingers stiffened. The smooth stem of the sherry glass slid through her hand. She heard the splintering tinkle as it smashed on to the flagged hearth. In horror, she looked down and saw the glittering shards of crystal, the wine spreading outwards in an uneven puddle.

'Oh, I am *so* sorry.'

'It doesn't matter, we've got dozens of them.' That was Mrs Kinnerton. 'Don't try to pick it up, anybody, you'll cut your hands.'

'I'll get a dustpan and brush,' said William instantly, and made for the door.

'In the kitchen,' Mrs Kennerton called after him. 'Ask somebody.'

'I . . . I don't know what happened,' Rachael went on apologising.

'I did that last week at a party,' said one of the other girls helpfully.

'Easy to do,' everybody agreed.

'Let's not talk about it any more,' decided Mrs Kinnerton, and went on, slightly flustered with her introductions, but Randall cut them short. Coming forward he said, 'Rachael and I know each other,' and he took one of her icy hands in his own, and kissed her cheek. He smiled. 'Hello, Rachael.'

'Well, isn't that nice?' said Mrs Kinnerton, slightly disconcerted. 'Now, darling, has everybody got a drink?'

'What are you doing here?' asked Randall.

'I'm staying with my cousin.'

'I had no idea you were in Devon.'

You weren't meant to. But she did not say this. She was still cold, trembling with nerves, and somehow it was difficult to think of anything to say. She only knew that she didn't want him here, in this house, in this room, at this party. She did not want him near. He was too attractive, too confident, he

26

had meant too much to her for too long a time. Why did fate have to play such a trick? Why couldn't she be left alone, in peace . . .

The girl in the flame chiffon came up and slid her arm through Randall's. 'I'm madly jealous,' she said, smiling, but not with her eyes. 'Who is this you are chatting up?'

'This is Rachael.'

'Hello. I'm Lucinda. Darling, I haven't got a drink and I'm longing for a cigarette.'

He gave her the cigarette and went to find her a drink. Lucinda puffed inexpertly into Rachael's face. Rachael wondered how old she was. Probably no more than nineteen.

'We're down for the weekend. For the races.'

It sounded very sophisticated. 'Yes, I know,' said Rachael.

'I've never been to Taunton before. I mean, I go to Ascot . . .'

Over her shining head Rachael saw William return from his visit to the kitchen, cheerfully bearing a dustpan and brush. Everybody stood aside to make room for him, and he proceeded neatly and deftly, to clear up the debris of the broken glass.

'I don't mind about the glass,' Mrs Kinnerton said again. 'It's the dogs' feet I worry about.' And she relieved William of the pan and brush, and bore them back to the kitchen.

William said, 'Rachael, don't look so agonised. It's all over. It didn't matter.'

'It was a dreadful thing to do.'

He went on gently, 'Are you all right?'

'Why?'

'You're so pale.' He took her fingers in his. 'And so cold.' His hand felt warm and comforting.

'I'm all right now,' she told him.

––•–•––

The evening, as unreal as an act from a play, progressed. After another ten minutes or so of chat, a gong rang somewhere and they all trooped across the chilly hall into a dining-room so large that the table in the middle was dwarfed into insignificance. There they stood about, expecting to be formally seated, but Mrs Kinnerton was busy ladling out soup from a huge cooking pot on the sideboard hotplate, and told them to sit where they wanted. William deftly pulled out a chair for Rachael, and then firmly planted himself next to her, but once the rest of them had sorted themselves out, he sprang to his feet and helped to hand around the soup. A plateful of steaming broth was placed in front of Rachael, and over her shoulder he said, under his breath, 'Scotch broth. Just the thing for icy shivers.'

The soup was followed by roast saddle of lamb and then apple fool and Devonshire cream. Mr Kinnerton, having tried politely to make conversation with the inattentive Lucinda, turned his attention to Rachael. He told her how he'd inherited the house from a cantankerous uncle. How his wife, almost single-handed, had turned the land from a wilderness into the famous garden it now was. 'Grew shelter belts, you know,' he told Rachael. 'Once you've got shelter you can grow pretty damn anything. Remember what it used to be like, William?'

Cheerfully, they reminisced. Rachael's eyes returned to Randall. Across the table he and Lucinda were talking, low-voiced, as though they exchanged intimate secrets. All evening, Lucinda had scarcely been able to take her eyes off him, or her hands. They seemed constantly to find reasons to touch him, to possess him. *I was like that*, Rachael told herself, without pride. *She is me all over again*. How many girls had there been before herself? How many would follow Lucinda? She suddenly felt tremendously sorry for the girl. Because she had it all in front of her; telephones that never ring, letters that never come. The agony of disappointment, the final heartbreak.

And Randall, the catalyst behind all this emotional upheaval. Randall, the charmer, irresistible to women. Sophisticated, but in many ways naive as a schoolboy. She saw him in the future, grown older, thickened by good living, his girlfriends becoming progressively younger. An ageing Peter Pan. She thought, *Poor Randall*. And this was astonishing, because the last thing she had ever imagined was herself feeling sorry for him. At that instant, as though she had said his name aloud, he looked up and met her eyes across the table. Lucinda was still murmuring away, but he did not seem to be listening to her. He simply looked at Rachael, and for a long moment neither turned away. And then Lucinda touched his arm, and his attention was diverted. He turned back to her and the tiny interlude was over.

And that, Rachael told herself, *was my last goodbye to Randall*.

They had driven for a long time in silence. As they came through Duncoombe the clock in the church tower struck one o'clock.

She said, 'I didn't realise it was so late.'

'Are you tired?'

'Not really.'

'Too tired to talk?'

'What about?'

'Why you dropped the sherry glass.'

Rachael said nothing. William brought the car around a steep bend in the road, and then, where it widened before them, drew into the side and turned off the engine. It was very quiet. Ahead, a new moon was rising up into the sky. William opened his window, and the smells of the country night drifted in on a wash of cold air.

He said, 'Perhaps you ought to talk. Perhaps now is as good a time as any.' He sounded as tranquil as ever. 'Why did you drop the glass?'

'I was taken by surprise.'

'By Randall Clewe.'

'Yes.' He did not comment on this, and his silence was encouraging, it made talking easy. She did not feel hurried nor driven into a corner. 'I knew him for a long time. I was in love with him for a long time. Then I said goodbye to him because I knew there wasn't any future – there wasn't any point in our going on. That's why I came to Devon to stay with Sally. To get away from Randall.'

'Are you still in love with him?'

She tried to say no, but found that she couldn't. 'I . . . I don't know. It isn't important.'

'Why isn't it important?'

'Because . . . I'm sorry for him. I'm sorry for him because he's going to go on thinking he's having a marvellous time, and actually he's not having anything. Just a sort of perpetual youthful jaunt. And one day he's going to wake up, and it's all going to be over, and he won't have anything to show for it. Except perhaps a string of scalps, and a lot of voices saying, "Randall Clewe – I was in love with him".'

After a little, William said gently, 'It's very difficult – almost impossible – for someone like me to understand the workings of the female mind.'

'You mean you didn't like him?'

'I suppose I have nothing in common with him.'

'Would you trust him?'

Again a pause, and then regretfully, 'No,' said William. 'Will you go back to London?'

'Sooner or later.'

'You wouldn't think of staying here, in Devon?'

Rachael turned her head and looked at him. 'What would I do here?'

'Marry me. I've loved you from the moment I saw you in Sally's shop. But you were so withdrawn, so cautious. There was a barrier there and I didn't know what it was.'

'William . . . I can't give you any sort of answer. Not just yet.'

'I don't expect you to. I just wanted you to know what I felt.'

31

'Oh, William . . .' She raised her hand and laid it against his cheek.

'That's a beginning,' he said. 'You're thinking about it, at least.' He took her hand from his cheek and put a kiss in its palm and then leaned forward and kissed her mouth. 'And that's another beginning.' He sounded content. He settled back into his seat, started up the engine once more. They moved forward and the lights of Tudleigh came into view, and far up the hill the lonely light over Sally's front door. It twinkled through the trees, across the darkness. A beacon, thought Rachael, and it felt a bit like coming into harbour after a long lonely journey.

Anniversary

It was a special evening. Yet disquieting, too, because Janey Ashcroft knew it, she couldn't be sure if David as well realised that it was special. That was how it was with them. A closeness, a rapport that was almost entire, except for these small niggling uncertainties which, most of the time, she was able to ignore, but sometimes, like tonight, grew like balloons to such size and importance that she wondered how she was going to be able to cope with them.

Because it was an occasion – for Janey at any rate – she wore her new dress, had washed her hair, brought a dozen chrysanthemums home from the shop so that the flat should look festive. When David arrived, crisp and cool-cheeked from the fresh evening air outside, she greeted him with a friendly kiss, and banked down the stupid disappointment that he had brought no present, no memento; and only realised in that instant that she had even vaguely expected such a thing to happen. Flowers would have told her that he remembered. Even one flower she could have pinned to her dress. Or a bottle of scent, or a little box to be taken from his jacket pocket and pressed into her hand: *Happy anniversary, darling.*

But nothing materialised. They simply kissed; he said she looked gorgeous. They went into the sitting-room, and it was full of the scent of chrysanthemums, and David, at home in this flat as he was in his own, poured a couple of drinks and sat himself in the armchair by the fire, and Janey sat opposite on a low stool, and they kissed again.

He said, sounding like anybody's husband, 'Did you have a good day?' And Janey told him about her day, which had been neither good nor bad, simply ordinary, with Miss Potter in a panic about flowers for the wedding next Saturday, and the delivery van breaking down in the middle of the main road, which entailed a dozen frantic explanatory phone calls.

'And you?' she prompted, sounding like anybody's wife, but with David, even disasters became funny. His detached description transformed the terrifying Sir Bruce into a comic character, turning the entire office upside down for the transcript of his vice-chairman's report, only to find it meekly sitting in the middle of his own desk. Janey laughed, and he added, sympathetically, 'Poor chap.'

'Was he apologetic?'

'No. Just red-faced, blustering slightly. You know the sort of thing.' He smiled at her. 'Where do you want to eat tonight?'

'I'm easy.'

'Gaston's?'

'Perfect.'

'Just as well. I booked a table.'

Of all the restaurants to which he took her, it was Janey's favourite. Small, French, informal. There were potted palms and mirrors, and the menu scrawled in chalk on a blackboard, and always the most marvellous smells of delicious food being prepared. They were welcomed with enthusiasm, shown to the usual table in the corner by the window, brought the menu and two glasses of sherry. Outside it had been breezy, and Janey took a mirror out of her bag in order to adjust a stray lock of hair. She smoothed it away from her forehead and looked up, over the rim of the mirror, to meet David's eyes. He raised his glass to her. He said, unbelievably, '*Happy anniversary, darling.*'

She could feel her face melt into an enormous, unstoppable smile. 'Oh, David.' She dropped the mirror into her bag, put out her hand, and his own closed over it, and held it close against the surface of the table.

'I didn't think you'd remember.'

'But you did.'

'Yes.'

'The first anniversary of the night we met. We've known each other for twelve months. Does it seem twelve months since that terrible party at Lucy's?'

'I had a cold.'

'And I hadn't wanted to go to the damn thing in the first place, but Lucy insisted.'

'You had an expression on your face that made you look like a boot.'

'I don't know why you spoke to me.'

'Only because nobody spoke to me. They must have been afraid of catching my cold.'

'I wasn't afraid. I must have been immune.'

Immune. She wondered if he was immune, not only to colds in the head, but also to this longing that Janey had for permanence. For a future with him. For . . . marriage. Just that. She wanted to marry David. She didn't care about weddings or white veils or bridesmaids or any of the conventional trimmings. She just wanted to spend the rest of her life with him. But David, for some reason, was different. David never mentioned the future. He never even talked about other people being married. With him, the subject simply never came up. Perhaps it was because of his own parents, who had divorced when he was a small boy. Perhaps it was because he didn't want to be tied down with responsibilities. Perhaps it was just that he had never met anybody that he loved enough. And that category, inevitably, included Janey.

Happy anniversary, darling.

A year. They had known each other a year. They had this closeness, this rapport. But the final certainty was missing, and it was this void that, because she loved him so much, she was learning to live with.

Over coffee he said, 'If it's fine on Saturday, let's go down to the country.'

'David, I can't.' He frowned. 'I told you. I'm going to Gloucestershire with my parents.'

His face cleared. 'The silver wedding weekend. You did tell me and I'd forgotten. In that case, I shall be dutiful and go and spend the day with my mother and sweep up her leaves.'

'I am sorry.' She could hardly bear to think of the next Saturday passing without their spending it together. Perhaps it would be raining, or brisk and sunny. She imagined a walk over the downs, lunch in a pub. He would wear a polo-necked sweater of incredible age, and Janey would have to run from time to time, to keep up with his long legs. She found, to her shame, that she almost wished the silver wedding wasn't happening.

She said, as much for her own sake as his, 'There'll be other Saturdays.'

'Of course. And twenty-five years of wedded bliss is something to be celebrated. Where are you staying?'

She told him. 'The Red Lion in Wittiscombe. They were there for their honeymoon. So it's all very romantic.' She hesitated for a second, trembling on the verge of the insane idea of asking David to join the party. Her parents had met him and liked him. Her mother in particular would be thrilled if he came. But . . . it was an insane idea. A silver wedding was no occasion to spring on a marriage-wary man, but rather to be treated lightly, with an attitude as casual as David's own. She said, 'At least it'll be a good excuse for them to get out on the Wittiscombe golf course and have a needle match. I just hope my mother doesn't win, or they won't be talking to each other by the evening.'

David laughed. She thought, *I'm getting quite good at this de-bunking lark.* And then, a little bitterly, *I've had twelve months' practice.*

Janey's parents lived in Bristol. The following Friday she duly caught a train to Cheltenham, where she was met at the station by her father. As soon as she stepped down off the train on to the platform, she saw him. Balding slightly, blue-eyed, wearing his tweed overcoat and an expression of cheerful anticipation. They hugged and he relieved her of her cases and she looked around and said, 'Where's Mamma?'

'We drove up this afternoon. She's already installed at The Red Lion. At this moment I expect she's soaking in a hot bath and relishing the thought of a dinner that she doesn't have to cook herself. She can't wait to see you.'

The family car was parked outside in the station yard. Mr Ashcroft loaded Janey's cases into the boot, and they headed out of the town and out into the country.

'Heaven,' said Janey, 'to get out of London. How are all the arrangements going for the great celebration?'

'Wait till I tell you,' said her father. 'Something splendid has happened. We're going to be joined by the Cressingtons.'

Janey digested this information, but it meant little to her. 'That sounds like the title of a play, and the name Cressington rings a bell, but apart from that I'm none the wiser.'

'Janey! You must have heard us talk of Bill Cressington. He was our best man.'

'Of course. How stupid of me. But then I've never met him.'

'How could you? He was always abroad, in Europe or South America or somewhere. He comes from a family with banking interests all over the world.'

'Lucky Bill Cressington.'

'And the extraordinary thing was that I met him quite by chance last week when I was in London for a meeting. Walked bang into him in the middle of Piccadilly, looking very tanned and handsome and pleased with life. He's just got back from a spell in the West Indies where he collected wife number three.'

'And did you know wives number one and two?'

'I suppose I met them fleetingly, but never for long enough to be able to say I actually knew them.'

'He sounds fascinating, but not really your type at all. How on earth did you meet him?'

'We were at university together. He was wild and wealthy and totally irresponsible, but so bright that he always managed to pass his examinations without appearing to do any work at all. A maddening man.'

'What does he look like now after all these years of riotous living? A bit seedy round the edges?'

'No, not seedy at all. He's good fun, Janey. You'll like him.'

'If you like him, then I shall too. And very satisfactory to have your best man at your silver wedding. It brings the whole business around in a nice, neat, full circle.'

———•◦•———

By the time they reached Wittiscombe, it was dark. The car came around the final corner and the main street lay before them, lamplit and lined with charmingly irregular gold stone houses. It curved up and away from them, leaning into the slope of the Cotswolds, and outside The Red Lion cars were parked on the cobbled ramp and light streamed out from uncurtained bow windows.

'All we need,' said Janey, 'is an unseasonable snowstorm and we've got a ready-made Christmas card. I always forget how marvellously picturesque this place is.'

They collected her bags and went inside, and the hotel was warm with log fires and welcoming smiles and people said 'good evening' and 'how nice' and the register was signed, and a lift bore them upstairs, and Janey was shown to her room which was small and looked out over the garden at the back of the hotel. There was a door into a private bathroom, and on the other side of the bathroom another door, which led into her parents' big double room, and there was Mrs Ashcroft, out of her bath and into her dressing-gown and enjoying what she called a toes-up on the bed.

She was reading a paper, which she tossed aside in order to open her arms to her daughter. 'Darling!'

Janey bounced on to the bed, and they hugged. 'Heaven to see you! Did Pa find you all right? Isn't it gorgeous here? So quiet. I'm going to revel in doing nothing, and not a meal to cook for three days. Did Pa tell you about the Cressingtons coming? You didn't see them on the way up, did you? They should be here by now.'

'No, we didn't see them. But I've been told all about them, West Indies, third wife and all.'

'She's bound to be gorgeous. He always had a taste for glamorous women. It's such fun, their coming. It will make everything sophisticated and slightly romantic, just the way a silver wedding celebration should be. None of us creeping around looking old, and Bill will flirt madly with not only his wife, but with you and me as well and we shall all feel cherished and beautiful. I can't think of anything nicer. Darling, tell me about London, and the shop. And . . . everything . . .'

Her voice trailed tactfully into nothing.

Everything, spoken in that tone, meant David. Mrs Ashcroft was painfully cautious about asking any questions. She never brought up David's name, she never interfered. But still, Janey knew. She replied, in a robust and casual tone which matched her mother's, 'Everything's ticking along. No problems.'

'You're looking thin.'

'Better than looking big.'

'You'll look big after this weekend. I've never seen such menus. And a special dinner laid on for us tomorrow night, and champagne on the house.'

'Do you feel as though you've been married for twenty-five years?'

'Sometimes it feels like fifty. And then I think of you as a baby and I wonder where all the years have gone.' She glanced at her watch. 'Heavens, I must get off this bed and go and do something about my hair. And then we'll go downstairs and see if we can find the Cressingtons.'

But they didn't have to look very hard, for the Cressingtons were already in the bar, waiting for them, and there was, in the midst of all the decorous pre-dinner sherry-sippers, an immense reunion. Kisses and hugs and introductions. Bill Cressington had obviously lost none of his glamour and revelled in the fact. Grey-haired, a little heavier than the stripling who had been best man at the wedding twenty-five years ago, he had a disconcerting expression in his eyes which would either madden or enchant a woman. In a dark suit, smoothly and expensively cut, a striped shirt, and a tie which could only have come from Rome, he radiated an aura of well-being which was as stimulating as a gust of sea-air. He told Mrs Ashcroft that she was more beautiful than ever; he appeared to keel over with delight at the very sight of Janey, and finally he introduced his wife.

'. . . and this is Tania.'

She was well-named. Janey couldn't imagine her being called anything else. She was quite young – perhaps twenty-eight, or twenty-nine, tanned from the West Indian sunshine, her eyes sky blue, her hair long and straight, falling like a silken curtain halfway down her back. She appeared to be wearing no make-up at all, but her lashes were long and thick and very black, and when she smiled her teeth were shining and white as a well-cared-for child's. She wore some sort of caftan, woven with gold threads which caught the light, and there was a gold bracelet at her wrist and gold rings in her ears. That was all, but she was simply the most spectacular girl that Janey had seen for a long time.

Tania said, glancing at her husband, 'I've never seen Bill so thrilled about anything. He was so pleased meeting your father in London that way. You know, after all these years, they just walked into each other in Piccadilly. It's the sort of coincidence I used to think only happened in books. But they do happen to Bill. All the time. It's the most extraordinary thing.'

'Then you don't mind being caught up in a sort of old boys' reunion?'

'Why should I mind?'

Janey looked over to where her parents and Bill were already deep in nostalgia. 'They're going to be doing this all weekend. "Do you remember old Miffley?" "And whatever happened to that girl with teeth you used to play tennis with?" You and I will be expected to listen and pay attention and laugh at all the right moments.'

'We don't need to,' said Tania comfortably. 'We can talk to each other. I'm sure you'd like a drink. What would you like Bill to order for you?'

That evening, dinner became so hilarious that Mrs Ashcroft, with a sympathetic eye towards the rest of the residents, kept saying 'Ssh'. Nobody took any notice of her. Over coffee they began to discuss how they would spend the following day. Janey's parents were determined to play golf. Bill obviously wanted to join them, but was charmingly considerate of his young wife.

'Darling, what do you want to do?'

'Play golf too,' Mr Ashcroft tried to persuade her.

'I can't,' said Tania.

'Neither can I,' said Janey.

'In that case,' said Tania, 'Janey and I will go and look at Wittiscombe Manor. It's open to the public and they have two Gainsboroughs and a Turner.'

Her husband surveyed her with the expression of a proud father, parent of a brilliant child. 'How did you find that out?'

'There's a notice in the hall, I read it while you were buying cigarettes.' She turned to Janey. 'Would you like that?'

'I'd love it.'

'It's only two miles away. We could walk there if it's a nice morning. And then Bill and your parents can play a three-ball foursome or a two-ball threesome or whatever it's called.' She smiled expansively around the table. 'So it's all arranged.'

———————

Saturday dawned cloudless, a little misty, but with the promise of a beautiful day. As the sun rose in the sky the mist was burned away, and the village lay golden and peaceful in the sunshine. After breakfast, Janey went out and sat on the steps outside the front door and watched her parents and Bill load the Ashcroft car with golf clubs and suitable shoes. Tania, wearing jeans and with her lovely hair tied up in an old silk scarf, had gone off to do some shopping. Now she could be seen coming back down the cobbled street towards them, holding out a brown paper bag out of which she was already munching a green apple. As she approached she explained this to Janey: 'If I'm going for a walk, I have to have apples to eat.'

Bill laughed. 'You know what you are, my darling? An apple alcoholic. It's a recognised disease.'

'If you're very good,' said his wife, 'I'll give you one, and you can eat it to cheer you up when you've missed all those two-foot putts.' He took an apple from her, put it in his pocket and gave her a kiss. Not a married man's peck but a proper kiss, on her mouth.

'What would I do without you?' he asked her, smiling down at her.

'I've no idea.'

'You're the most beautiful girl and I love you.'

'For that,' she said, 'you can have another apple. For the other pocket.'

They were ready at last. Janey and Tania stood, waving, until the car was out of sight. Then Janey said, 'What a super husband.'

'Why do you say that?'

'So appreciative and unselfconscious, kissing you in the middle of the street. Most men would rather die than do that.'

'But he's always like that. And he makes me laugh and he's so marvellous to live with.' They turned and began to walk up the gentle slope of the street. 'You know,' Tania went on, 'it's no secret that he's been married twice already, but I simply can't imagine why any woman would leave him. They must have been out of their minds.'

'When did you meet him?'

'About a year ago. I was working in the West Indies helping to run a boutique.'

'Had you always lived out there?'

'No, I sailed out there in a yacht with three chaps. I was meant to be the cook, but I wasn't much good at it.' She threw away the core of her apple and helped herself to another.

'Where do you live now?'

'In London. We've got a flat there.'

'Don't you miss the West Indies?'

'Only on horrible days. And I'd rather be in London with Bill than in the West Indies without him.' She tipped up her face to the sun and took a great sniff of fresh air. 'And this is better than either of them. Goodness, I'm glad we came!'

They walked on. As they left the village behind them, Wittiscombe Manor revealed itself, high on the hill above them, caught in a fold of the Cotswolds, its narrow chimneys spiring above the foliage. The road wound up the slope, and there were random cottages, where children played Saturday-morning games in gardens aflame with dahlias and chrys-anthemums. But when they came at last to the Manor, they met with disappointment. For although the gates stood open, and the drive curved temptingly away from them through the trees, a notice announced that the house was closed.

'How maddening,' said Janey.

'Never mind,' said Tania. 'Let's just go anyway.'

'But we can't.'

'We'll pretend we never saw the notice. Come on. We can't do any harm.'

It was like being at school; being wickedly brave because the other girl was braver than you were. 'Well, if we're accosted by a furious gardener, you'll have to talk us out of it . . .'

They went up the drive, and presently the trees opened out and the old house slumbered before them, ageless, time-less, smothered in Virginia creeper and set in lawns which sloped away down to a ha-ha wall and then a little park.

Cows grazed in the park. They seemed to be the only living creatures around.

They came to the house and stood, looking up at its beautiful, irregular face. There was an immense oriel window and a crest carved in the stone over the door.

'I don't even know the name of the family who own the place,' said Tania, but words were scarcely out of her mouth when, in front of their astonished eyes, the door began slowly to open, and a little woman stood there, wearing a brown dress and a pink apron. She had fuzzy white hair and spectacles and she said, 'Good morning.'

Tania was not in the least disconcerted. 'What a lovely day.'

'I saw you come up the drive from the bedroom window. There's nobody home. The family's away.'

'I'm afraid we're just rubber-necking. You know. Sightseeing.'

'The house is closed.'

'Yes, we saw the notice. We just came to look at it. We'll go away now.'

But Tania's charm was irresistible. The housekeeper, or whatever she was, hesitated only for a moment. Then she said, 'Well, the family's away, like I said. Do you want to come in? I could show you around.'

'Oh, that would be lovely. If you're sure it's not too much trouble.'

'No. No trouble. I'd be pleased to. Come away in.'

And so, after all, they saw the house and the Gainsboroughs and the Turner. And they were shown the family drawing-room, and the room where Queen Elizabeth had slept, and when the guided tour was over, the housekeeper took them into the kitchen and made them a cup of tea, and then told them that if they wanted they could go out at the back and have a wander round the garden.

Tania said, 'Are you sure?'

'Of course. You won't do no harm. I can tell. I'm not one to be mistaken about people.'

'You are kind,' said Tania and, when they had said goodbye, she gave the housekeeper a kiss, quite naturally, as though they had known each other all their lives.

The garden was as delightful as the house. They strolled through a maze of rose-beds, into a wild garden where a magnolia of immense age spread its branches over a tangle of marigolds, love-in-the-mist and vivid blue lobelias. Lawns climbed behind the house in a series of terraces, and the girls went right to the top and found a stone summer house, and there sat in the sunshine with all the Vale of Evesham spread out before them. There was only birdsong to be heard, and the occasional drone of a distant jet.

Tania began to eat her last apple. She said, abruptly, 'I love your parents.'

'Yes. They're nice.'

'Are you going to get married?'

The question, disconcerting, was neither inquisitive nor curious. Simply interested.

'I don't know,' said Janey. She had been trying not to think about David all day.

'But there's someone special?'

'Yes.'

'Don't you want to get married?'

'Yes, I'd like to.'

'But he doesn't want to?'

'I don't know.'

'Aren't men hell?' said Tania sympathetically, and finished her apple in silence and threw the core away. Janey waited for her to say something more, but she leaned back against the stone wall of the summer house, and turned up her marvellous face to the sun. Her eyes closed. Her lashes lay like dark fans against the tan of her cheeks. Watching her, observing her was a pleasure. She charmed; she was beautiful; apparently flawless.

———•◦•———

That evening, after she had changed, Janey went into her parents' room and gave them their present. A photograph of herself – which had been asked for – in a silver frame – which had not. They were gratifyingly pleased. There was even a shine of a tear in her mother's eyes. 'We couldn't have had anything nicer,' she told Janey. 'And we couldn't have had a nicer daughter. We're really terribly lucky.'

Mrs Ashcroft wore a new dress which her husband had given her, and her pale curly hair framed a face which was as excited as a child's. Growing old seemed suddenly not too ghastly a prospect. In fact, it could be fun if you did it in the company of the person you most loved. Janey thought of David and knew that to be without him, even on this happy family occasion, was like being only half alive.

She smiled quickly, to drive away the stupid lump in her throat, the stinging behind her eyes. She said, 'I'm lucky, too.'

It was a splendid evening. The dinner was perfect, the champagne delicious, there were roses on the table, a few telegrams from friends, and Bill made the perfect speech. In fact, it was Bill and Tania who made the evening. But then, thought Janey, watching them laughing and flirting together, teasing her parents, charming the waitress, Bill and Tania were the sort of people, glamorous and vital, who would turn any occasion into a memorable celebration.

<hr />

The next morning Janey was wakened from sleep by the telephone ringing by her bed. Muzzily, she stretched out a hand and picked up the receiver. Muzzily, she said, 'Hello.'

A male voice said, 'Are you asleep?'

After a little pause, Janey said, 'David?'

'Yes, it's me.'

'What time is it?'

'Eight o'clock. I'm sorry to wake you, but I thought, perhaps . . . I mean, if it's all right . . . I might drive down and have lunch with you all. And then I could drive you back to London and you wouldn't have to catch the train. Would that be a good idea?'

'Oh, David, the best!'

'Your parents won't mind me horning in?'

'They'll be thrilled.'

'How did the party go last night?'

'It was a tremendous success. The Cressingtons are here. He was my father's best man. He's got a glamorous wife and they're really super. Oh, David, I can't think of anything nicer. Ring off now, and get into the car and start driving.'

'I'll be there about one.'

'We'll wait for you.'

Waiting for David, the morning seemed endless. She spent it eating a slow breakfast, and packing her case, and then walking up to the village shop to buy a Sunday paper. Her parents had gone to church and returned about twelve, and the Cressingtons joined them, and they all went into the bar for an aperitif, but Janey stayed outside, near the front door, so that she would see David the moment his car drew up outside the hotel. The day which had started brightly had degenerated sadly into rain, but that didn't matter. It was a beautiful day because David was on his way to her.

He came, as he had said he would, just before one. She went out and they met on the steps and he kissed her, and he was wearing her favourite shirt, and a cashmere pullover and light fawn trousers which made his legs look very long and lean. She was very proud of him. She took him into the bar, and he had brought flowers for her mother, and a bottle of champagne for her father; and when she had introduced him to Tania and he had turned away for a moment to tell Mr Ashcroft what he would like to drink, Tania hissed in Janey's ear, 'Is that the one?' and Janey made shushing noises and nodded her head furiously, and Tania mouthed 'He's smashing!' and they both began to laugh like a pair of school-girls.

After lunch, when everyone else had gone off to pack, she and David went for a little walk, up on to the hill behind the village. It was still raining, but the wind had got up and the showers came in gusty squalls and blew Janey's hair all over her face and whipped a healthy glow into David's cheeks. And when they came to the top of the hill they found an abandoned cottage with a stream running through the garden and an old mill wheel, and because it had stopped raining for a moment, they sat, side by side, on an old log which happened to be lying around, and listened to the sound of rushing water and the shiver of the wind in the trees, and there didn't seem to be any need to make conversation.

After a while, Janey said, 'Perhaps we'd better get back. I have to say goodbye to my parents before they go . . .' But he put his hand on her arm, restraining her. She looked into his face and something that she saw there made her ask, 'What is it?'

He frowned. 'I've been thinking.'

'About something important?'

'Yes. Important. Yes, it is important.'

She waited. 'Do you want to tell me, or do you just want to go on thinking?'

'I have to tell you, because it's about you.' He leaned down to pick up a handful of small pebbles. As he spoke he played with them, dropping them from one hand to the other. 'It's about you, and my own parents, and your parents and, in a roundabout way, the Cressingtons. It's about a small boy listening to his parents quarrelling through the wall, or running out into the garden, and putting his hands over his ears so that he wouldn't hear them shouting at each other. And after the divorce, going from one to the other, listening to long tales of woe, trying not to take sides. And it's about seeing your parents today and realising that after twenty-five years they still laugh at the same jokes. And it's about the Cressingtons. But they've got it too, that magic which ought to exist between married people, and which I was beginning to think simply didn't exist.'

'Oh, David.'

'It's nothing to do with boyhood traumas or cynicism. It's just that you get asked to some wedding, and there are white veils and morning coats and all the right hymns, and a month later you're asked for dinner and everything's fine; and then a couple of months later you meet them again, and she's griping because he's late at the office, and he's griping because she won't give up her job, or she won't get a job or something. There'll be some idiotic bone of contention, and they'll be tearing each other apart over it. And then in a couple of years, likely as not, they're separating or splitting up, and all you can pray is that there aren't any children to get fouled up in the works.'

She did not at once reply to all this. It was difficult to think of anything to say. After a little she sighed and said, 'I had no idea you felt as strongly as this.'

'I never told you. And I never wanted it to end like that with us. I wanted it to go on for a long long time. And I wanted it to start like the Cressingtons. He's old enough to be her father, and he's been married before, I know, but still, they've got something special going for them. They look at each other and it's like there's nobody else in the room. And even if he's talking to you, his eyes keep going back to her, as though he had to keep reassuring himself of his own good fortune. They don't hide their love away as though it were something to be ashamed of. They don't spend their time finding stupid nit-picking issues to quarrel over.' As he spoke his face was very serious, a frown furrowed between his darkly-marked brows. But now, looking down at her, he suddenly smiled. 'After we're married, you won't go looking for nit-picking issues, will you?'

Janey said faintly, 'I wouldn't know one if I saw one.'

'We will get married, won't we?'

'Yes, please.'

'I'd have asked you months ago, but I had to be sure of my stupid self.'

'You're sure now?'

'Never been more certain about anything.'

'It's the same with me.'

'Then I'll take you back to London and buy you a great big vulgar engagement ring. And we'll break the news to our respective families.'

'But not today. Let's keep it to ourselves for today.'

'All right. Whatever you say.'

It began to rain again, but they never noticed. He pulled her into his arms and pressed his cheek against hers and the rain ran down his hair on to her face, and his old tweed jacket smelled of peat smoke, and she knew it would always remind her, that smell, of this moment, when she was filled with more happiness than she had known in her life before.

———◦———

When they got back to the hotel, her parents were on the verge of departing. They were only waiting for Janey and David to return, they said, and Janey's mother looked at David and then at Janey, and then back at David again, but Janey said nothing. She just hugged her mother, and said it had been the best weekend she had ever spent. And the Ashcrofts got into their car without any more delay, and sped away, arms waving goodbye from the two rolled-down windows. And Janey and David waved back, watching until the car turned the corner and was out of sight.

David looked at her. 'We should start off, too. Are you packed and ready?'

'Yes. My cases are in the hall.'

'I'll get them.'

'I'll just go up and say goodbye to Bill and Tania.'

'Yes, you do that, and I'll load my car.'

Indoors, the hotel was heavy with the slumberous Sunday afternoon. From some distant lounge the television could be heard, and in the back kitchen someone clashed beer crates around. Janey went upstairs two at a time, and along the passage to the Cressingtons' room. She knocked and Tania called, 'Come in'; Janey opened the door and saw Tania, alone, occupied in packing what looked like four suitcases at the same time. Since lunch she had changed into her jeans and her long hair was tied back into a careless tail and secured with a piece of pink wool.

'Janey!'

'I just came to say goodbye.'

'Bill's gone off to see an old friend who lives nearby. He's left me to cope with all the horrible packing.' She smiled. 'Don't you hate the end of weekends?'

They had said, *let's keep it to ourselves for today*, but finding Tania alone suddenly prompted Janey to break this resolution. Tania, of all people should be told about herself and David. After all, the Cressingtons, as a couple, had provided the catalyst that had finally opened David's eyes, and given him the courage to face the truth that marriage was not necessarily synonymous either with boredom or disaster. She took a deep breath and began, 'I've got something to tell you . . .'

But that was as far she got, because Tania interrupted her. 'I've got something to tell you, too.' Janey waited, taken unawares by the other's abrupt tone of voice. Tania sat on the edge of the bed. She said, 'I wasn't meant to tell you, but I like you too much, and after yesterday, and the weekend and everything, for some reason I feel as if I've known you all my life. And I hate lying to people I like.' Janey stared at her. Tania looked up and said, 'We're not married. That's all. We're just not married.'

Janey felt her face drop in sheer disbelief. 'You . . . you mean . . . ?' her voice tailed off into nothing.

Tania nodded. 'Just that. We're not married.'

'But . . .' she thought of Bill. 'But he adores you. You adore each other. You told me yesterday. Why not be married?'

'It just never comes up.'

'But he's divorced, isn't he?'

'I don't know.'

Janey felt cold with shock. 'But you want to be married to him, Tania, surely. Don't you want that?'

'I'm not even sure of that. We seem to have just slipped into a situation that's beyond both of us.' She frowned. 'Don't look so miserable. You mustn't be unhappy. I only told you because, like I said, I hate lying to people I like. But don't say anything to your parents, or Bill will kill me.'

'Of course I won't. But, Tania . . . what's going to happen to you both?'

'I haven't any idea.' For a frightening moment Janey thought that Tania was going to cry. But she was wrong, because the next instant Tania was smiling. Once more her lovely face lit up, artless, the eyes such a bright and shining blue. 'Anyway, now you know. I'm glad you do. And what were you going to tell me?'

'Oh. It's gone right out of my head. It couldn't have been very important. I really came to say goodbye.'

'We'll see each other again.'

'Of course.'

'I'll be in touch.'

They kissed, gave each other a hug. Tania went back to her packing and Janey left her, closing the door between them. Outside, she stood for a moment, she felt shaken, incapable, as though the ground had given way beneath her feet. Without seeing where she was going, she went down the Turkish-carpeted corridor, past the lift and the potted palm and started down the stairs. On the turn of the staircase, she stopped. David was waiting for her in the hall. As she appeared above him, he looked up.

'Did you see them?' he asked.

'Just Tania.' She descended to his side. 'Bill's out seeing a friend.'

'What did Tania have to say for herself?'

Janey stopped on the bottom stair. Her eyes were level with David's. She said, 'Nothing. Just goodbye.'

It was the first lie she had ever told him. But, in his car and heading back for London, she promised herself that one day she would tell him the truth. Maybe next week. Or the week after that. But not today. Today was too soon.

Skelmerton

I heard the boy before I saw him. The reason for this was a sea mist which had come in from the east like a cloud of grey smoke, sliding along the sand as though it were being blown beneath a door; cloaking with alarming speed the sea, the sky, the beach, the dunes. What had been a world of bright spring sunshine was blotted out by a fog which tasted of salt. The sparkling waves, racing across the sand on the flood tide, were reduced to a sullen, distant booming. Inland the mist poured in and devoured the pleasant landscape of brown plough and green pasture and beech trees, just coming into leaf. It was suddenly very cold.

I was on horseback. In case this sounds rather grand, I must explain quickly that the horse was a shaggy pony, called Daisy, at least three sizes too small for me, belonging to a small girl called Isobel. Isobel, on being sent to boarding school, came to me close to tears to ask if I would sometimes exercise Daisy for her. Otherwise Daisy would get fat, would eat too much, go off her legs and finally explode. Isobel didn't say so in so many words, but her agonised tones led me to understand that nothing was beyond disastrous belief.

I promised that I would do as she asked, and accordingly bicycled up two or three times a week, captured Daisy in what always seemed to be the most distant corner of a field, saddled her up in her shabby equipage and took her for a decorous ride. By 'decorous' I mean that we didn't gallop along the shore pretending to be a television commercial, nor did we jump five-barred gates, but it was a pleasant way of passing an afternoon and we both enjoyed it.

Anyway, there we were, on an early April afternoon riding along the sands when the mist came in. Or 'fret' as they call it in Northumberland. Daisy, being Northumbrian born and bred, was no more spooked by the fret than I was, but continued placidly on her way until we came to the rocks which mark the end of the bay.

We could not see these rocks, but there was the tang of seaweed, and the hiss and rumble of the flood tide moving in beneath the cliff. Fulmars nested on these shallow cliffs and the clammy air was rent with their strange cries. Daisy splashed through a deep sand pool and up on to the hard sand on the other side. The cliffs reared up before us, sinister in the fog, and I said to Daisy, 'This is as far as we come,' and started to turn her when we heard the cry. It could have been a fulmar. I stopped and listened, and it came again.

'Hello–o–o . . .'

Daisy's ears pricked. We stared into the fog, saw nothing.

'Where are you–ou–ou?'

'Here!' I called back, and my voice sounded unfamiliar and puny and was lost in the echoes of the cliff face.

There came a scramble of falling stones. Daisy, uneasy of the unknown, whickered anxiously. I laid a hand on her neck, and her shaggy coat, beneath my palm, was beaded with damp. We waited, both straining our eyes and ears.

A movement through the fog; another stone rattled over rock, and the next moment, as though from nowhere, a figure appeared, took shape, not ten feet from where we stood. A small boy wearing jeans and a blue sweater, apparently soaking wet and totally alone.

'I couldn't see you,' he said reproachfully. 'I heard you coming, but I couldn't see you at all.'

'Are you lost?' I asked.

'Well, I wasn't till the mist came in, but I am now.' He was perhaps eight years old, not particularly tough-looking but quite self-possessed.

'Are you alone?'

'Yes, I came down for a walk. Mrs Skelmerton said it would be all right, but not to be too long. But then I found some crabs in a rock pool and I was looking at them, and the next thing I knew it was all horrible and foggy.'

'Are you staying with Mrs Skelmerton?'

'Yes, do you know her? Will you show me how to get back to her house? I don't mean to take me back. I mean just show me on to the road and then I can find the way.'

'Of course I will.' He seemed very small and wet. 'Do you want to ride?'

He looked doubtful. 'I shouldn't think your pony could take the two of us.'

'I'll walk, and you can ride.'

'Oh, no, that wouldn't be fair.'

'In that case—' I dismounted – 'we'll all walk. You and me and Daisy. She'll think this is her lucky day, going back to her stable without anything heavier on her back than a saddle.'

He said, 'Can I take her reins?'

I handed them to him. He handled them competently, a child used to ponies. We moved off, three abreast, Daisy's hooves making a pleasant sound on the hard sand.

I said, 'You should watch out for the fret. It can be dangerous if you get caught on the cliffs, specially with the tide coming in.'

'Watch out for what?'

'Fret. That's Northumbrian for sea-mist.'

'Do you know other Northumbrian words?'

'Some. Country words. Do you live in the country?'

'No, London. We lived in America for a bit, but we live in London now. I'm here for a week, staying with Mrs Skelmerton. It's nice, but the house is so big. I don't much like my bedroom either. You keep thinking there might be ghosts.'

'I don't think Skelmerton's that sort of a house.'

Around Daisy's placid nose, the boy looked at me suspiciously. 'How can you be sure?'

'Because I have lived here all my life. And I'm sure I'd have heard if there were ghosts.'

'Where do you live?'

'In the village.' He was quiet for a little, probably still thinking about ghosts. To change the subject, I asked him his name.

'I'm William. But most people call me Tiger. I'm even called Tiger at school. It's funny, because I didn't tell anybody I was called Tiger. They just seemed to know.'

'Why are you called Tiger?'

'I don't know.'

'Perhaps you were a very fierce baby and bit people?'

He gave this due consideration. 'Oh, I shouldn't think so.' He thought some more. 'Anyway, babies don't have teeth for ages.'

There was no question of having to find our way home. Daisy led us like a homing pigeon, up and over the dunes, along the paths which had been trodden to mud by grazing cattle, through the gate and up the lane which led to the village.

Here, half a mile or so from the sea, the mist thinned out a little and the village street revealed itself to us, wet and empty. Tiger looked up and down, and then said, 'Now I know where I am. I can find my way back now.' He handed me the reins and tipped back his head to look up into my face. His eyes were dark as blackberries, his soft hair plastered wetly to the shape of his skull. He said, 'Thank you so much.' He smiled. And it was then that I knew who he was.

———•◦•———

Skelmerton is a small village. It has one large house, one medium-sized house and a lot of old stone cottages. The large house is Skelmerton Manor where old Mrs Skelmerton lives alone in shabby grandeur, surrounded by a tangled garden and a small park filled with grazing cattle. The largish house is called The Shrubberies and is owned by the Priestly-Browns who are newcomers, having only lived in the village for ten years. Mr Priestly-Brown works in Newcastle, commuting by train each day, and Mrs Priestly-Brown is a woman of immense energies and confidence. She runs everything she can lay her hands on, and when she has been particularly maddening I tell myself that she is also pretentious and condescending. My father, however, merely points out that she is hardworking, generous and deeply concerned with the community as a whole. But then he is a clergyman and the medium-sized house is the rectory, where we live.

The cottages are simply cottages, with small windows crammed with net curtains and potted geraniums. One or two of them have been bought up by other commuters who have built on garden extensions, or thrown out picture windows, but not enough to spoil the look of the place.

All in all, it is a very nice village, and my father has been rector of St George's, Skelmerton, for fifteen years. He also looks after the parishes of Abbots Whelper and High Houghton which involves, on Sundays, a fairly tight schedule and a good deal of nippy driving. He is a very good priest; I think because he has a sense of humour.

When we came to Skelmerton, my mother was alive. It was she who turned the Rectory from a gloomy, chill mausoleum into the charming, sun-filled house it is now. It was she who created the garden out of a neglected wilderness; tore out all the old laurels and felled the monkey puzzle trees, and planted azaleas and silver birches which stand, in springtime, knee-deep in a carpet of daffodils. I always think that a garden is the best sort of legacy a person can leave. When she died I was in

London, nursing, and everybody said, 'You can't give it up. You can't go home.'

But I did anyway and I've lived in Skelmerton ever since.

———•◦•———

That day of the fog, when I finally bicycled up the short drive that led to home, I saw Mrs Priestly-Brown's car at the door, and my heart sank. I put my bicycle away, went up to my room to change and tidy up, taking as long about it as I decently could, but when I came down she was still there, perched across the hearthrug from my father with the fire blazing merrily between them and the warm air filled with the scent of the blue hyacinths which I had planted last autumn.

She was a small, slender woman (no one so energetic possibly put on weight), always dressed with immense chic, never glimpsed without lipstick, pearls and nail varnish. Her hair was grey, discreetly blued, never a curl out of place. She always made me feel a mess, however hard I tried.

'And here's Caroline!' she cried, as though I were about to do some sort of trick. 'Had a nice ride, dear? Your father and I have just had a good long chat about the summer fête. Just as well to get it cut and dried without a lot of people interfering.' Perhaps this sounded, even to her ears, a little close to the wind, so she added swiftly, 'Not that everybody in the village doesn't work like a slave when the time comes, but there's such a lot of groundwork to be put in first.'

I looked at the clock and said, 'Have you had tea?'

'Oh, ages ago.'

'A glass of sherry then?'

'No, I won't, thank you all the same. I must be off. But first . . .' she sprang to her narrow feet and stooped to pick up a businesslike bag which bulged like a briefcase . . . 'I want you both to come and have a drink at The Shrubberies tomorrow evening. About six o'clock, just one or two people, not a proper party, quite impromptu.'

My father muttered something about impromptu parties always being the best.

'That's what I told Mrs Skelmerton. I was up at the Manor today, collecting for the children's home . . .' (I could imagine her in the Skelmerton drawing-room, oozing charm and rattling her tin. I suspected that, like the rest of us, she was rather in awe of Mrs Skelmerton, but that didn't stop her ruthlessly name-dropping) '. . . and the idea occurred to me then.' She turned to me. 'You will come, won't you, Caroline?'

She had an expression on her face which I knew well. Not just on Mrs Priestly-Brown's face, but on the faces of other match-making ladies. *Poor Caroline*, it said. *Twenty-seven and living at home with a parson for a father. What chance does she have of meeting anybody? We must be kind to her.*

'I'd like to,' I murmured.

She went on, with an arch light in her eye. 'She has the most charming man staying with her.'

I said, coolly, 'Is he called Leo Walton?' It was astonishing how easy I made it sound, how casual.

'Why . . . yes. How did you know?'

'He came to Skelmerton a long time ago. Ten years at least.

We met him then.' I turned to my father. 'You remember him, don't you?'

'Yes, of course.' He can be marvellously bland. 'But, Caroline, how did you know . . . ?'

'I thought I saw his son on the beach this afternoon.' And I wanted to add, for Mrs Priestly-Brown's benefit, *Leo Walton has been married for ten years to a beautiful girl called Cynthia, and he has a little boy called Tiger, who has inherited his father's smile.*

But of course I didn't. And the next moment Mrs Priestly-Brown said, '*Poor* little boy.'

I frowned. 'Why so poor?'

'You can't have heard. And why should you? Mrs Skelmerton only told me this afternoon when she was showing me out to my car. I said, what a charming man, and she said yes, and brave too. And I said, why so brave, and she told me – so tragic – that his wife had been killed in a car crash about a year ago. It happened in America; he was working out there for his firm. They were so devoted to each other she said.' She looked at my father. 'Sometimes one hears of such things happening and one wonders *why.*' At the expression she saw in his face, she floundered a little. 'Of course, I know there doesn't have to be a reason. At least not a reason we mortals can understand. But . . .'

He took pity on her. 'Yes, I know. And we had no idea about Leo's wife. Thank you for telling us.'

She cheered up a little. 'And I can expect you both tomorrow?'

'Yes, of course,' my father began, but I interrupted. 'I've just remembered – I shan't be able to come after all, I have to go, and . . .' I cast about frantically for inspiration, '. . . have tea with Deirdre,' was all I could come up with.

My father gazed at me in open disbelief. Deirdre is a dim girl who was at school with me. She lives in a gloomy house out beyond Rothbury and I have been heard to say that I would rather be found dead than spend half an hour in her company. He said, at last, 'How nice.'

'Oh.' Mrs Priestly-Brown looked gratifyingly disappointed. 'Can't you put her off?'

'No, not possibly. I am sorry, but it's really impossible. Poor Deirdre. She doesn't have much of a life with that old aunt.' And Mrs Priestly-Brown said no, of course not, but did not sound convinced. And she took herself off, obviously deciding that not only was I twenty-seven and unmarried, but in imminent danger of cluttering up what remained of my life with Good Works.

———◆———

I was seventeen when Leo Walton came into my life. I had finished school and when Mrs Skelmerton phoned to ask if I would like to go up to the Manor and play tennis with some young people who were staying with her, it made me feel marvellously grown-up, which just shows what an innocent I was. I had a new tennis dress, very short, which showed off my tan, acquired as the result of an unexpectedly hot spell of weather. I had to bicycle up to the Manor as I hadn't yet passed my driving test, but even that didn't dampen my good spirits.

As I came up the drive I saw that a knock-up was already in progress on the old hard court that was apt to sprout this-tles in unlikely places. I got off my bicycle and parked it incongruously against the great curving stone balustrade of the front steps, and was about to make my way down to join the rest of the party, when a voice spoke behind me.

'Hello.'

I turned and looked up. He had appeared from the front door and was coming down the steps towards me. He wore jeans and a striped cotton sweater and a pair of very old, dirty tennis shoes. His hair was very dark, his face tanned, his eyes unexpectedly light beneath darkly-marked brows. He was smiling. He said, 'You must be Caroline.'

'Yes, I am.'

'Mrs Skelmerton told me to look out for you. I'm Leo Walton.'

I said, 'How do you do?' and fell in love.

I suppose that sounds very old-fashioned. But that's just the way it happened. One moment I was just Caroline, the person I had always known, living a life without surprises or secrets. The next instant my entire existence had altered; had taken on new dimensions, new horizons. I had been headed one way, now I moved in a totally different direction. Being in love with Leo was a new universe and he was its axis, and around that axis I was to spin for ever.

He said, 'You look very professional, I expect you'll knock us all off the court.'

I had been captain of tennis at school, but I only said, 'Not really.'

'I didn't come prepared for tennis and I hoped that my lack of equipment would be good reason to sit and spectate, but the delusion was swiftly dispelled. These shoes belonged to the late Mr Skelmerton and they're at least three sizes too big, and smelly to boot.' I began to laugh, and he laughed, too, and said, 'Come along, we mustn't keep the others waiting.'

———•·•———

It was the beginning of a wonderful week. One thing led to another; the tennis party to an enormous barbecue on the beach, and the barbecue to an expedition to Dunstanburgh. Here Mrs Skelmerton, like some ancient warrior, led us up crumbling towers in the teeth of the east wind, and stood, pointing with her stick and treating us all to a lecture on rounded bastions, fortifications and garderobes. And it was fun because Leo was part of it all. Everybody liked him. The fact that I was never alone with him didn't bother me in the least. In fact I decided, if I did find myself in such a situation, I should be scared stiff and become utterly tongue-tied. But I was wrong. Because one morning I was waiting for the bus to take me to Alnwick where I had promised to do the weekend marketing for my mother. As I stood there, propped against the bus shelter and making up fantasies about Leo Walton, he suddenly appeared alongside me, sitting behind the wheel of a dashing red car. He said, 'Where are you going?'

'To Alnwick.'

'Hop in, then; I'll take you.'

I hopped in, the basket on my knee. He put the car into gear and we zoomed off, through the village, up and over the hill. It was a bright morning with a south-west wind, and the sky was blue, ballooned with great banks of white cumulus which cast scudding cloud shadows across the face of the moors.

He said, 'What a view.' He smiled at me. 'And what a fantastic place to live.'

'Where do you live?'

'In London. I work there, so I live there.'

'Have you known Mrs Skelmerton for long?'

'All my life. She was a friend of my grandmother's. I used to come here when I was a boy. But you weren't here then. There was a different rector.'

'Yes, I know.'

'Now you've left school, will you stay here?'

'No. I'm going to do nursing. I think.'

'Where?'

'In London.' Another fantasy took shape. I saw him asking me for my address, coming to take me out to dine in some glittering spot, driving me down Park Lane in this very car.

'Any particular hospital?' he asked.

'I don't know yet. I've got to go down and have interviews.'

'It's hell, isn't it, trying to ease your way into some sort of profession? It's so easy to make some mistake at the very beginning and then you get in a mess, and you have to go back to the beginning and start all over again.'

I said, 'Like Ludo.'

'Or Snakes and Ladders.'

He only had to go to the gunsmith's for some fishing tackle, and I had a list that would take me an hour, but he said that he would wait and drive me home, and that I would find him in the bar of the Swan. I had never been into the bar of the Swan in my life. In fact I had never been into a bar but I wasn't going to tell him that, and when I had finished the shopping I just walked in as to the manner born, and he was waiting for me, sitting on a high stool and reading the newspaper. I said his name, and he stood up and folded the paper. 'Put the basket down and tell me what you want to drink,' he said, and I asked for a glass of cider, and he had some beer, and we sat together in the gloom and the stuffiness of the little bar, it seemed the nicest place I had ever been.

I did not see him again until the Sunday. I don't go to church every Sunday, my father being the open-minded man that he is, but this particular Sunday I felt rather like it even if it was only to pray with enormous fervour that Leo should continue to like me for ever and ever.

Our pew was at the very back so I sat there watching everybody coming in. Just five minutes before the service was due to start I heard a car arrive outside, the sound of voices.

The next moment Mrs Skelmerton marched in like a general at the head of his troops. Behind her, dutifully, came her house-party from the Manor. I waited for Leo, and he brought up the rear, but with him was a girl I hadn't seen before. She was hatless and her hair was dark and curly, and she wore a red skirt and a nut-brown velvet jacket that I would have given anything for. Leo never saw me. But as I stared at their backs the girl turned up her head to whisper something to him, and he bent his head the better to listen, and his hand cupped her elbow. There was something about the tender possession of his touch that turned a cold knife in my heart. I had never been jealous before and to experience it now, for the first time, in church was the most terrible thing that had ever happened to me. But I couldn't take my eyes off them, and as she turned to make her way into the Skelmerton pew I saw her delicate profile, the sweep of her lashes, the blackberry darkness of her eyes.

She was called Cynthia Ross, and three months later Leo married her. I never spoke to her, because that morning I was first out of church and halfway home before any of the rest of the congregation had shifted from the pews. And that evening I heard that she and Leo had gone back to London together. And I never saw him again.

———

I never loved any other man, but in ten years you can learn to live with almost anything, and slowly I accepted the fact that I had lost him, and the years passed by and I knew that he had probably forgotten all about me. On this basis, I had been prepared to meet him again, to go to Mrs Priestly-Brown's, to shake hands, to say 'How nice to see you again,' to be introduced to his wife, and to smile into the dark eyes which had looked up at me from the rain-washed face of her small son. And we would perhaps sip a sherry and remember that long-ago time, and laugh about the late Mr Skelmerton's tennis shoes, and Mrs Skelmerton's guided tour of Dunstanburgh.

But now? Now it was different, Cynthia was dead, and for some reason it seemed to me that both Leo and I were hideously vulnerable. I could not bear the idea of his being sorry for me, as people, for some reason, were. And he would be defensive and changed and I would find it difficult to know what to say to him. I imagined him trying to be breezy. 'Hello, Caroline! What have you been doing with your life?' And perhaps he would take pity on me, even if it was only to take me out and feed me in some hotel. And once he had done this and his conscience was clear, he would take himself off and I would be left with the old wound open and bleeding. And I couldn't go through all that for the second time.

So instead of going to Mrs Priestly-Brown's I spent a tedious evening with Deirdre and her aunt and that, I imagined, was the end of it. But I had reckoned without Mrs Skelmerton.

The morning after Mrs Priestly-Brown's party, she hailed me in her fog-horn voice across the village street. I was posting a letter, and she was coming out of the butcher's, weighed down with parcels which were large enough to contain sirloins but were more likely dog food.

'Caroline! Wait, my dear, I want to talk to you.' She opened the door of her old shooting brake, tumbled the parcels in, slammed the door, and shot across the road to my side, narrowly missing death at the wheels of a small passing van. 'Why weren't you at the Priestly-Browns last night?'

She stood there, stringy and tanned like a length of old rope, her white hair on end, her tweeds lanky, her lavishly-darned stockings wrinkled and sagging around her bony shins. At my age I should be able to cope with Mrs Skelmerton, but she has always terrified me and she always will.

'I . . . er . . . I had to go and see a friend.'

'Your father told me. That poor Deirdre girl. You know you could never stand her. And I know it, too. You'll have to think of a better excuse than that.'

'Excuse?' I said faintly, trying to bluff.

But she was not to be bluffed. 'Just what I say. You know I've got Leo and the youngster staying with me. You know he's lost his wife. Such a pretty little thing she was, too. And don't try to tell me that you didn't like him. I haven't forgotten you, laughing and chattering away, that day I took you all to Dunstanburgh. So . . .' her disconcertingly clear eyes bored into mine. 'What's it all about? Running away. That's what it's about. Sheer selfishness, if you ask me. And it's about time you learned that running away doesn't do any good. So come to Skelmerton tonight. Yes, another party. I've asked a good many people already and I want you, and your father too, if he can tear himself away from the Mother's Union.'

'Well . . . I . . .'

'Six o'clock!' It was an order. 'And don't you dare not to come.'

I knew that I would not dare. I walked home, angry to begin with and then, slowly, becoming less angry. I might have known that those eyes missed nothing, that nothing that she considered important was ever forgotten. And by the time I had reached home I knew that she was right. Running away didn't solve problems. It was time for the fantasies to be forgotten, and the past decently buried. Leo was no longer a young man and I was twenty-seven. All at once, for no reason, twenty-seven seemed a good age to be. It had both a past and a future, and yet I was still young. And even if that future was never to include Leo, it was still mine; personal and unique to me as the colour of my hair, the shape of my eyes, my finger-prints. This gave me a comforting sense of identity, of destiny, as though there were nothing I could not overcome.

———•◦•———

I went alone to the party because my father was occupied with a confirmation class. I wore a long skirt and a little braided jacket and a white shirt with the neck tied like a hunting stock. And I piled my long hair up into a chignon and secured it with a tortoiseshell comb, and I splashed myself with the best of my scent and picked up my bag and went downstairs. Outside, it was a beautiful evening, cold and with a crisp breeze, but a sky above of clear blue was already pricked with the first of the stars.

My father had kindly walked to the confirmation class

and left the car for me; I got into it and drove to the old house which waited, timeless, square-faced, random light shining from the windows. The great beeches which stood about made a pleasant soughing sound in the wind from the sea, but the gravel sweep in front of the house was empty of cars, and I wondered if I was very early. I got out of the car and went up the steps, lifting my long skirts, and through the door into the flagged hall. It was a very cold house and chill seeped up from the flags, and a thin draught drifted down the staircase. There was no sound except a certain clattering from the back regions, but the drawing-room door was ajar. I went towards it and pushed it open and saw the big, shabby room, the logs smouldering in a bed of ash in the great hearth, the books and magazines scattered about, a bag of untidy knitting. And Leo alone, deep in a sagging armchair, reading a paper. Like the room, he did not look as though he were expecting company, being dressed in a pair of hard-worked-looking corduroys and an elderly green sweater.

He heard me come in, and he lowered the newspaper and looked up, and across the room, across the years, we faced each other. I saw that he was now quite grey-haired; there were lines about his eyes and his mouth that had not been there before, but still the immense attraction was there, the pale eyes and the dark brows, the shape of the mouth . . .

I said quietly, 'Hello, Leo.'

He dropped his paper and pulled himself out of the chair. 'Caroline!'

I looked around at the unattended room and said, resignedly, 'There isn't any party.'

'Why were you expecting one?'

'Your hostess is a shameless liar.'

'You mean she told you that there was going to be a party?'

'She said she'd asked a good many people. I should have known she had something up her sleeve, the old conspirator. And now I look a total fool, all dressed up and nowhere to go.'

He said, 'You look fine,' and he laughed and I realised that Mrs Skelerton's outrageous behaviour had given us a talking point and the ice was broken between us. 'And if she is a shameless liar, then she'll have had good reason. Like getting hold of you. I thought I'd see you last night otherwise I'd never have gone to that nattering woman's. There wasn't a soul there I knew.' He pulled himself together then, and became a host. 'Now come along in and shut the door and get close to the fire. I always forget what a hellishly cold house this is, despite the warmth of the hospitality. And as you've been asked for a drink, I think I should give you one.' He went over to a table laden with odd bottles and glasses. He picked them up, reading the labels on the bottles with an expression on his face which did not bode well for the contents. 'Sherry seems the safest.'

'Sherry would be perfect.'

He poured two glasses and brought them over. We drank to each other. He said, 'So many years. So much water under the bridge. Tell me what happened to you. What happened to the nursing?'

'That was a long time ago. I started but I never finished. My mother died and I came home to keep an eye on my father.'

'Mrs Skelmerton told me. It seems a shame.'

'No, not a shame. And I have a feeling I couldn't have lasted for ever working in London.' He was easy to talk to. He had always been easy to talk to and now he watched me, the pale eyes very kind and understanding, but not sorry for me in any way. Not saying, *Poor Caroline*. I said, 'And you, Leo?'

'You knew that Cynthia was killed?'

'Yes, I heard. I'm so sorry.'

'We were driving back to New York from Connecticut. She was driving. There was black ice on the road and the car skidded.' He shrugged. 'All finished in a single instant.'

'You came back to this country?'

'Yes, my job out there was finished anyway. And it was better coming home. It's helped Tiger come out of it, given him new things to think about.' He thought about this. 'Tiger is having a bath and he's coming down for his supper which is baked beans. Mrs Skelmerton's in the kitchen now, heating them up on the Aga.'

'Why is he called Tiger?'

'Cynthia called him Tiger. To go with Leo. But he's really named William . . .' He was about to tell me more but at this moment, like a well-managed stage play, the door burst open and the young man in question made an explosive entry. He wore an unevenly-buttoned dressing-gown and his damp hair stood on end.

83

'Daddy, are my beans ready, because there's something super on television . . .'

Then he saw me and stopped dead. His face dropped into an open mouth of delight and astonishment. I had never felt so flattered in my life.

'It's you!' he shrieked.

'Hello, Tiger.'

'Have you come to see me?'

'Yes, and your father and Mrs Skelmerton. And I thought a lot of other people, but I was mistaken.' Leo was staring at us both with incomprehension all over his face, so I put him out of his uncertainty. I said, 'I should have told you. Tiger and I have already met.'

'I *told* you,' said Tiger. 'I told you about the lady on the beach who rescued me from the fog.'

'You mean . . . this is the same lady?'

'I've just said, haven't I?'

Looking at me, Leo shook his head. 'How ridiculous,' he said. 'I never realised it was you. Tiger told us all about his adventure, but I never realised it was you who brought him home.'

'And I couldn't tell Daddy your name, because I never asked you what it was. And I tried to tell everybody what you looked like so that they would know, but everybody was so stupid . . .'

'I'm sure they weren't,' I began tactfully, but I was interrupted by a hoot like a hunting horn from the back regions of the house, which was Mrs Skelmerton letting Tiger know that his supper was ready.

'You'd better run along and eat your beans,' advised Leo.

Tiger looked at me. 'You won't go? I'll come back when I've finished them.'

'I won't go.'

Tiger left us. Still standing by the fire, we turned towards each other. Leo said, 'He's been talking about you ever since the day of the fog. And the reason we were so dense as to the identity of his rescuer is that his description of you was charmingly but not strictly accurate. Long blond hair, right down your back, and eyes the colour of the sky, and mounted on a snow-white steed.'

There came a ridiculous lump in my throat. I managed to say, 'It's gratifying to be thought of that way.'

'I think,' said Leo, 'that he must have fallen in love with you, he certainly remembered you with the eye of love.'

I said, 'I knew who he was. He didn't say, but when he smiled I knew who he was. He's inherited your smile, Leo. It's a good thing when you can recognise a son by his father.'

He said, 'Caroline, do you remember that pub in Alnwick when I took you for a drink? If we telephoned and booked a table, do you think they would rustle up a dinner for us? I suspect that Mrs Skelmerton would be glad to see the back of me, and then she can eat the rest of Tiger's baked beans for her supper and watch television without having to be bothered by me.'

I said, 'That's the most gracious invitation I've ever had.'

He grinned. 'And what about your father? Can he look after himself?'

'For one evening I think he could.'

'That's settled then.'

'But Leo . . .'

I stopped. He looked down and saw the expression on my face. He said gently, 'What is it?'

'I don't want you to feel . . . I mean . . . that you have any obligation . . .'

Mercifully, he overrode my mumblings. He said, 'I have only a happy remembrance of things past. And I am grateful to you for making friends with Tiger, who needs a little female companionship very badly. Is that enough to be going on with?'

'Yes, of course.'

'So we'll have dinner together, and talk about old times.'

'Yes,' I said. 'Yes, I'd like to do that.'

So we did.

So that's how it happened. And that was only yesterday. Now it's the next morning, and I'm waiting for Leo and Tiger, because the three of us are taking a picnic lunch to Dunstanburgh. So I don't yet know how our story's going to end. We'll just have to wait and see. As my father would say, we are in the hands of the Almighty.

A Place Like Home

Joanna Crayshaw, twenty-six years old and lately relieved of her appendix, sat up in the hospital bed and pretended to read the magazine the woman in the next bed had lent her.

It was visiting time, the middle of the afternoon, and the woman in the next bed had a whole family of visitors; a son, a daughter, and a chubby grand-daughter with a doll dressed in wonderfully hand-knitted clothes. The woman in the next bed was called Mrs Wilson, and Joanna was sure that she had knitted the doll's clothes for the little girl's birthday. She looked that sort of kindly person, and her family sat about on chairs, smiling proudly and talking nineteen to the dozen. The daughter had brought Mrs Wilson a clean nightdress, the son a tin of shortbread. They were obviously devoted to the white-haired lady, whose plump and comfortable folds of upper arm and bosom were tastefully draped by a lacy wool bed-jacket. Her best, she had told Joanna as the nurse helped her on with it. Only the best would do for her family. She sat up, expectant, waiting to arrive.

The little ward was full of visitors and family chat, and Joanna felt conspicuous because she had nobody. But there was nobody to come and see her. Her parents were dead, her only sister in Philadelphia and Aunt Cassie, in whose rambling Surrey house Joanna usually spent the weekends, had gone off to Florence for a little holiday with her friend Helen. They had been to Florence together as girls and had been looking forward for months to this nostalgic jaunt around the great galleries. Aunt Cassie didn't even know Joanna was in hospital. The appendix operation had been one of those emergency affairs, and there was always the possibility that, on receiving the news, Aunt Cassie might hot-foot it back to England, which would be a cruel shame. No, better for her to find out when she came home in the normal way. By then Joanna would be out of hospital and in need of a little cosseting.

She turned the page of the magazine and read there how to pack for a summer holiday; how to tan gradually, how to make a useful beach bag. The efforts implied made her feel exhausted. She was glad that she did not have to go on holiday. She was glad she had no visitors. Her scar was tender and her eyes felt heavy with tiredness. She laid down the magazine and began to slip down under the sheet, carefully, as though it were important for no one to notice.

Sister was coming down the ward towards her, her rubbery shoes squeaking on the polish of the shining floor.

'A visitor for you,' she said. Joanna realised, in some dismay, that she was talking to her. Behind Sister came a man, tall, balding, dark-suited, at first vaguely familiar and then, surprisingly, totally familiar. 'Isn't that nice? You've got a visitor after all.'

He came to the foot of the bed. He said. 'Hello, Joanna.'

'Mr William!'

He was William Anderson, the senior partner of Anderson's Trading, and Joanna's boss. She could scarcely have been more astonished, and yet, deep down, she found that she was not astonished at all. It was typical of the man that he would leave his busy office at three in the afternoon and come across London to see how a very junior member of his staff was getting along.

Nothing was too much trouble for Mr William and he had built up a reputation throughout the firm simply by his attention to detail, his perfection. A woman, not even a regular customer, would write to him from Cumberland requesting that he produce a large terracotta pot from Provence to adorn her newly-constructed terrace. And Mr William would go to work, leaving no stone unturned, until the exact pot was run to earth, purchased and conveyed to the customer's rural address.

It was the same with everything else. The shop sold Japanese umbrellas, French cooking pots, Venetian glass, Persian rugs, English china, American bed-linen and the most beautiful Scandinavian furniture, but still Mr William would take infinite pains to match up a chintz or a dish, to have made a lampshade the exact blue of a lamp-base, to find a craftsman capable of engraving some precious piece of presentation crystal.

He was perhaps thirty-seven, but looked older, his eyes a gentle blue behind the formidable spectacles. His clothes were formal and usually a little old-fashioned. He had never been heard to raise his voice, and any admonishments that were necessary always took place privately and behind closed doors.

Consequently his staff adored him and stayed for years. Joanna had worked for Anderson's for three years, first in the soft goods and then in the glass and china department. She was a very small cog in a big machine, but that made no difference to Mr William, and to prove this, here he was, pulling up a chair to her bedside and laying a small bunch of freesias on the white cotton bedspread.

'I thought you'd like the smell,' he said.

'Oh, delicious!' Her most favourite flowers. How could he have guessed they were her favourite? She took a deep sniff and was instantly transported back in time to her father's garden when she was a child, and the greenhouse, sun-drenched and steamy, where he had grown freesias and cultivated a vine that hung with bloomy fruit.

She looked up. She said, shyly, 'You really shouldn't have bothered.'

'Of course I bothered. You gave us all a terrible fright. How are you feeling?'

'A little tender, but I'm all right.'

'Sister said you've had no visitors.'

'No. My aunt's in Florence on holiday. And my sister's in the States, her husband is doing an exchange job with the university in Philadelphia.'

'Does she know you're in hospital?'

'I wrote to her this morning.'

'And where will you go when they discharge you?'

'Aunt Cassie should be back by then. I expect I'll go to her. She lives in Surrey.'

Mr William considered this, his expression thoughtful. Embarrassed by the silence, Joanna smelled the freesias again. He said, choosing his words carefully, 'I think you should have a little holiday. Get right away.'

The word holiday made her feel exhausted. She imagined crowded airports; grappling with luggage, heat, for foreign languages, the sort of hotels that look like hen batteries. She said, faintly, 'I don't think I've got the energy.'

He did not appear to think this was a stupid remark. He continued to survey her thoughtfully. And then he said, 'Have you ever been to Scotland?'

She said, fearfully, 'No.' Scotland conjured up even more fatiguing images. Of cold and rain, and having to climb steep hills, or stand waist deep in running water trying to catch a fish. She had seen photographs.

'Then why not go to Scotland for a week or so? It's a most restoring place.'

'I don't know anybody in Scotland.'

'But I do. Don't forget, I hail from north of the Border. I have some great friends, Mr and Mrs Duffy. They live on a farm, in the country. They would be so pleased to have you to stay with them.'

Joanna eyed Mr William with suspicion. 'How do you know they would be pleased?'

He smiled. 'Because I have already spoken to them on the telephone. So will you think about it?'

She said, 'Whereabouts in Scotland?' as though it could make any difference.

He told her, 'Near Relkirk. You could go by train. Someone would meet you at the station. Very civilised,' he added, encouragingly, perhaps seeing the doubt on her face. 'I'd like you to see the place where I was born and brought up. The farm is called Whitebarns and the countryside is very peaceful and beautiful.'

This was a new side to Mr William. 'I never thought of you as a country boy.'

'I came to London when I was nineteen. That's a long time ago. But my roots are still in the north.' He stood up. 'You'll think about it?' he said again, and because he had taken so much trouble, Joanna said that yes, she would.

———⋅◆⋅———

'Was that your boyfriend?' asked Mrs Wilson when the visitors had gone.

'No, he's my boss.'

'Oh, your *boss*.'

She sounded coy, Joanna firmly nipped any rumour in the bud. 'He's married, and he has three children.'

Mrs Wilson's face fell. She had scented a romance. To cheer her, Joanna said, 'He wants me to take a holiday in Scotland.'

Mrs Wilson was intrigued. 'I went there last year on a coach trip. Lovely it was, except that it rained the whole time. Are you going to go?'

'I don't know,' said Joanna. 'I don't suppose I will.'

But of course she did. Aunt Cassie was enjoying Florence so much that she wrote to tell Joanna she had decided to stay out there until the end of the month. And by the same post came a letter from Mr William enclosing her rail ticket and a generous cheque 'to cover expenses'.

The Duffys are expecting you and much looking forward to your visit. Willie Duffy will doubtless meet you at Relkirk station. Have a good rest and let me know when you want to return to work, but not until you are quite strong again.

And he remained hers, sincerely, William Anderson.

Joanna folded the letter and put it back in the envelope.

'Are you going to Scotland?' asked Mrs Wilson.

'Yes,' said Joanna.

It was late summer. The train drew out of a Euston sweltering in airless heat which had accumulated at the end of a stifling day. It drew into Relkirk at seven o'clock on a cool and pearly morning and the air through the opened window of Joanna's carriage smelled of real air, as refreshing as a long drink of cold water.

She was going to be met, Mr William had promised, but how Mr Duffy would look was a complete mystery. She got out on to the platform and the sleeping-car attendant lifted down her cases, and she stood there, waiting to be claimed and feeling mildly panic-stricken. She was always wary, at the best of times, of meeting new people. But the station had a country air which was reassuring, with a crate of chickens loaded on to a trolley, and a tweeded man collecting his dog from the luggage van where it had spent the night. The dog was a golden

Labrador, and so delighted to be free that it tore about in excited circles.

'Are you Joanna Crayshaw?'

Startled, she turned from watching the dog and found her eyes on the level of a blue, open-necked shirt. They travelled up to the face of an extremely tall young man. It was a sunburned face, with very blue eyes, topped by a thatch of reddish fair hair. His expression was that of a man prepared to go as far as was necessary in the cause of good manners, but no further. Friendly but reserved. She felt slightly chilled, but told herself that there was no reason why he should be delighted to see her.

She said, 'Yes, I am. How clever of you to know.'

She sounded gushing, even to herself, and perhaps he thought she sounded gushing too, because his expression didn't soften. There was a small uncertain hiatus which ended in their shaking hands.

'There wasn't anyone else got off the train who could possibly have been you,' he said, and picked up her suitcase.

His voice was unmistakenly Scottish. Joanna said, almost running to try and keep up with his long legs, 'Are you Willie Duffy?'

'No,' said the young man. 'Willie couldn't come. One of the cows is sick and he's waiting on the vet.'

There didn't seem to be any comment to make on this, so Joanna said nothing. She was half-expecting him to introduce himself, but such social niceties appeared to be beyond him. She began to wonder if he was shy or merely rude, but could only follow him past the ticket barrier, and out into the station yard, where he strode over the cobbles to a waiting Land Rover, heaved her case over the tailgate, and opened the door for her.

———·•·———

She climbed in, looking about her. A street of Georgian houses led down from the station yard towards an open park with large, leafy trees. A bridge curved over a ribbon of water and beyond were hills, rising softly to other hills.

He clambered up beside her, slammed the door shut, started the engine. She said, 'What a pretty town,' but he only said, 'It's all right,' and let in the clutch and they were away.

It took only minutes before they were in open country, a wide, flat valley of fields and lanes and trees, sparsely dotted with farmsteads. Sometimes these buildings were white, sometimes a deep terracotta. Cattle grazed peacefully and tractors were out at work.

The silence between them was not exactly strained, but even so it could not go on forever. Joanna glanced sideways at the strong-featured profile and decided he had an ungiving face.

She took a deep breath and tried again. 'Do you work at Whitebarns?'

'Yes.'

'Do you work for Mr Duffy?'

'Not exactly.'

'Do you know Mr William Anderson?'

This time, a slight inclination of the head. 'Yes, I know him well.'

Joanna battled on. 'Do you live with the Duffys?'

'No, I'm away on my own.'

She decided that he was hopeless and stopped trying. The countryside was infinitely more rewarding. Now, there were fruit orchards and fields of raspberry canes. The Land Rover bumped over a level crossing and then ran down a straight lane between hawthorn hedges, and stopped before a small cottage, single storied, with a neat garden and a blue front door.

'Here we are,' she was told.

'Here?'

She had not meant to sound surprised, but had never imagined a dwelling so modest. The young man blew a blast on the horn, a dog started barking and then the front door opened and a woman came out with a sheepdog at her heels. She had reddish hair, turning white, and a blue apron over her green and white dress.

'So you're Joanna Crayshaw, and here you are safe and sound. And I'm Mrs Duffy. So Bob found you all right. Now, can you bring her case in, Bob? You must come this way and I'll show you your room. Willie's away out to see the vet, but I thought that you would maybe take a bite of breakfast . . .' Inside, the house was larger than it first appeared because at some time a modern kitchen and two extra rooms had been added to the back. Mrs Duffy showed Joanna into one of these rooms, which had a window looking out on the orchard, and there was flower-ed wallpaper, and white cotton curtains, which were blowing in the morning breeze. Mrs Duffy made clucking noises and was about to shut the window.

Outside the door Bob's voice called, 'Where shall I put the case?'

'In here.' He appeared, ducking his head cautiously in this house which had been designed for folk much smaller than himself. 'That's it, just there in the corner,' Mrs Duffy said.

Bob set it down and straightened. 'I'll be off then,' he said, hovering in the doorway.

Joanna pulled herself together, and turned from the delights of the view.

'Thank you very much,' she said, 'for coming to meet me.'

'No bother.' He smiled. The smile was disarming and took her unawares. Joanna suddenly realised that she had enjoyed the last half-hour in the company of a handsome and personable man.

'Bye, Minnie,' he said to Mrs Duffy and took himself off. The Land Rover roared away down the lane.

Then Minnie Duffy said, 'He's a good boy, and no mistake. Mind, he's a different cup of tea from Bill, a different man altogether. A real country boy, but he has a mind of his own. If he has a fault, it is that he's backward in coming forward. But tell me, now, how is Bill? And the children? It seems a long time since we've set eyes on the dear wee souls.'

Joanna was disorientated. She said, quietly, 'Bill?'

'Mr William Anderson. Of course Mr Duffy and me have known him since . . . he was a wee thing. Since Duffy started here, as cattleman, twenty-five years ago or more . . .'

She chattered on, and Joanna, listening in horrified disbelief, realised that the taciturn Bob was none other than Mr William's younger brother. That he was the owner of Whitebarns, and far from working for Mr Duffy, he actually employed him. Thinking of the gaffes she had made, the questions she had asked, made Joanna feel quite hot with embarrassment.

She said, 'I had no idea who he was. Why didn't he tell me?'

Minnie Duffy shook her head. 'That Bob! Isn't it just like him not to introduce himself? He'll be the death of the lot of us one day, with his close ways. But it was funny Bill didn't put you a wee bit more in the picture, as they say.'

———•◦•———

A day went by and a second, and a third. The sun, obligingly, shone. Joanna stayed in the cottage garden, pretending to read a book, or helping Mrs Duffy thin her lettuces. Later, when she felt more energetic, she took undemanding walks down the flat lanes between the orchards.

More adventurous still, she finally walked to the river, swollen to a great estuary two or three miles wide. Here the water was tidal and the mudflats inhabited by a marvellous variety of birds. Peewits nested in the marshy seafields and there were flocks of black and white birds that she could not identify.

She was sitting at the edge of the grassy shore, watching them, wishing that she had binoculars, when she heard a dog barking up on the slope behind her, and a man's voice, and she turned and saw coming through the open gate at the top of the slope a herd of black cattle, harried by a dog, and being driven down by none other than Bob Anderson himself.

Joanna's heart sank and she dithered as to what she should do. Pretend she hadn't seen him? Stand up and wave? Or walk up the grass to meet him and risk a possible snub?

The cattle scented the fresh grass, decided to stop being frisky and peacefully began to graze. Bob whistled, and the dog scampered back to his side. She watched him come through the gate and close it behind him. He started down the slope towards her and after a moment's hesitation, Joanna went to meet him.

He waited for her, one foot braced against the slope of the grass. He wore an elderly tweed hat, pushed on to the back of his head, and a pair of jeans washed and faded to the palest of blues.

He did not smile, but said, in quite a friendly way, 'How are you getting along?'

'I'm all right, thank you.'

'Is Mrs Duffy looking after you? Feeding you all right?'

'She's being marvellous. I shall be so fat by the time I get back to London I shan't be able to get into any of my clothes.'

'You could do with a bit of fattening up,' he said, as though she were one of his cows, but Joanna did not feel insulted. In fact, she was delighted, because they seemed to have embarked upon what could almost be termed a conversation.

———◦◦◦———

Encouraged, she said, 'You know, I never realised you were Mr William's brother. You probably guessed I didn't realise it.'

'Minnie Duffy said I should have told you myself. But I

don't know, I never thought much about it.' He obviously didn't seem to think that the confusion of their first morning mattered at all, and if he didn't think it mattered, then why should Joanna? 'Did you walk down here? That's quite a way. You must be recovering.'

'I was looking at the birds. I know the peewits. But the big black and white ones . . . ?'

'They're shelducks. Beautiful birds. But not as beautiful as the greylags, the wild geese. They're here for the wintertime. Arrive on the twenty-first of September, give or take half a day or so. And they stay all the winter and go back north in the spring. Hearing them fly over, on a cold morning, honking and talking away to each other . . . it's one of the best sounds ever.'

She said, 'I wish I had a bird book.'

'I've got a book at the house. If you like I'll lend it to you.'

'Would you?'

He had a long crook with him. Now he set this into the ground and leaned his chin on the carved horn handle. He said, 'Tell you what, come along to the house this evening, and I'll give it to you.' Joanna looked at him. His eyes were very blue, quite friendly. Ulterior motives did not appear to lurk behind them. And she was disarmed by his friendliness. She said, 'I'd like to.'

'About seven then.' With this settled, he straightened up. 'I've got the Land Rover here in the field. Do you want a ride back?'

But Joanna said she liked the walk and so, with the dog at

his heels, he left her, and she went back to watching the birds and told herself that he was just being neighbourly.

In the Duffy's house the evening meal took the most splendid form, High Tea. At half past five a pie was produced, or minced beef, or fried haddock, to be followed by home-made scones and butter, sugared cakes and endless cups of tea. Joanna wondered how Mrs Duffy had managed to keep her neat shape after a lifetime of such spreads. That evening, when she had helped Mrs Duffy with the dishes, she set off, armed with a gingerbread as a present for Bob, to walk across the orchards to the farmhouse.

It was a beautiful evening, very still and scented with the sea-smells of a flood tide. Whitebarns stood perhaps half a mile from the Duffy cottage, and was screened by trees. As she approached, Joanna saw the steading, the barns, the high wall built around the garden. The door into the house stood open, and she stepped into a flagged hallway from which rose a charming staircase. There was a cool, scrubbed smell, rather like well-kept dairies.

She waited. 'Is anyone at home?' she called, and the dog barked, and the next moment Bob emerged from a door at the end of the hall and came to greet her.

'You found your way?'

'It wasn't too difficult. And Mrs Duffy sent you this.' She gave him the gingerbread.

'That's very kind.' He took it. 'Now, would you like a cup of coffee or a glass of lager or something?'

'I'd love some lager . . .'

'I thought we'd go out into the garden. It's still warm.'

He poured the lager neatly, and handed Joanna the glass. He said, 'I found the book. It's on the chest in the hall, so don't forget and go back without it.'

'It's so kind of you . . .'

'How much longer are you going to be here?'

'I think about a week.'

'You're looking better. A different person to the girl who got off the train.'

'I still feel badly about that day.'

'No cause to feel badly. It was my fault. Bill always said I should take a course in making friends and influencing people. He said if I didn't watch out, I'd win the prize for the rudest man in the county.'

'I can hear him saying that.'

'You know . . . I don't know anything about you. Except that you work for William.'

'That's about all there is to know.'

And then, because this sounded a little bleak, she enlarged on it. 'I mean there's nothing very interesting. I have a flat in London that I sometimes share with another girl and I work for Anderson's Trading, and that's about it.'

'I can't believe it's as simple as that.'

'I'm afraid it is. Would you like me to pretend my life is seething with intrigue?'

He said, very seriously, 'I wouldn't want you to pretend anything.'

His calm voice, his steady eyes, somehow caught her

unawares. She knew a moment of panic, and to change the subject she said, in a voice bright with interest, 'Have you always lived at Whitebarns?'

'Yes, man and boy.'

'Who looks after the house for you?'

He grinned, suddenly looking young as a boy. 'Minnie Duffy has already told you I haven't got a wife?'

Joanna had to laugh. 'Yes, she has, but I can't think why?'

'I say I have never found a girl to match up with me. And I didn't say match up to me, I said match up with me. And my brother Bill says it's because I take so long to make up my mind about anything that by the time I asked a girl to marry me, she'd be already happily married to somebody else and like as not expecting her third child.'

'So you have a housekeeper?'

'I've got a young pig-man; his wife comes in and cleans for me.'

'Did the farm belong to your father?'

'Yes, and my grandfather before him. William was the eldest, and by rights the farm should have come to him, but he was never cut out for farming. He was the artistic type, always had his nose in a book. So when he left school he went south and joined my uncle in Anderson's Trading in London. It's funny, two brothers like Bill and me. So different, but that doesn't mean we don't get on well. Never saw much of each other after he went down to London, but when we did, it was as though we'd never been apart.'

'It's good when you feel like that about someone. I think

he's one of the nicest men I've ever known – coming to see me in hospital, and arranging for me to come away and stay with the Duffys . . . nobody else would have been so concerned.'

'Perhaps,' said Bob, 'the fact that you have no parents makes him feel more than usually responsible.'

'I wouldn't want to think that.'

'Why not?'

'Because I want to feel that I'm standing on my own feet.'

Bob smiled. He said, 'And where were *you* brought up?'

'In Dorset. Hardy country. My father was a solicitor. We had a country house in the middle of a town – it had high walls all around and the garden always seemed to me the safest and most secret place in the world.'

'Is your sister older than you?'

Joanna frowned. 'How do you know about my sister and my parents?'

Bob went a bit red in the face. 'I had a wee chat with Minnie . . . I wasn't just curious, I was interested.'

Joanna forgave him and said, 'She's older than me.' She remembered the smell of freesias in hospital, and somehow it was like a million happy memories suddenly coming flooding back. She began to talk, telling Bob about the greenhouse and the vine; and the summer tennis-parties with school-friends. And Christmases with charades and candlelight and going on holidays to North Wales, all of them packed into her father's modest car. She said, 'We used to camp, in tents, and one year we hired a caravan but somehow it was never so much fun as sleeping in a tent.'

'What happened to your home?'

'We sold it when my mother died.'

'Do you ever go back?'

'No.' She thought about it. 'Nor talk about it.' She looked at him. 'This is the first time I've talked about it. I've never wanted to before.'

'It's your family makes a home,' said Bob. 'They make it a special place.'

———————

She realised in some astonishment that it was growing dark. The midges were starting to bite, and Bob slapped one off his hand and suggested that perhaps it was time to take Joanna home. He said that he would drive her in the Land Rover, but it was still so warm that she elected to walk, and he walked with her, across the fields and beneath the bloomy shadows of the old pear trees. In the distance could be seen a light in the window of Mrs Duffy's house, and very yellow and cosy it looked, welcoming Joanna home.

Home. That word seemed to be ringing through this strange evening, like the persistent tolling of a bell. 'It's your family makes a home,' Bob had said, meaning loved ones, familiar faces, security. Why then, in the middle of this unknown country, did she suddenly feel, for the first time in years, that she really belonged? Not to the flat in London, which was merely a place to return to after a day's work. Not to Aunt Cassie's house, which she visited at weekends. But here. Now. This was the place.

She had stopped walking. She stood still and looked up through the leafy boughs of trees, to the infinite, misty arc of the evening sky. She saw the new moon, fine as an eyelash, rising up over the ragged silhouette of the hawthorn hedge, and heard, from the river, the gentle cackle and chatter of nesting birds. A few paces ahead Bob stopped and waited for her.

'What's wrong?' he asked at last.

She did not reply. After a little he came back to her side, his shirt pale in the faint light, his sunburned arms and face merging strangely into the dusk. He ducked his head beneath a drooping branch and she watched him, and realised in an earth-shattering instant that the security, the feeling of belonging, emanated not from the little lighted window but from him. She thought, *Dear heaven, I can't have fallen in love with him . . .*

He said her name, but she didn't reply because she couldn't say anything. He reached her side, and took her shoulders between his big hands, and pulled her towards him, and now there was nothing to be said by either of them, because he was kissing her as though he couldn't bear to let her go.

They met again at noon the following day. Bob had his 'piece with him', which meant that he had brought a sandwich and a Thermos of tea out into the fields, and Mrs Duffy had made Joanna a picnic. They had arranged to meet by the river, and she was waiting for him down on the shore when she heard his voice, his whistle, the bark of the dog, and she looked back, and there he was coming through the gate, and this time there was no hesitation. She ran to meet him and he picked her up and swung her around and set her down and said, 'You haven't changed your mind?'

'Changed your mind about what?'

'About you, about me, about last night?'

She said, 'I love you,' and that seemed to answer all his questions.

They made their way back to the water's edge, or at least what would have been the water's edge if the tide hadn't happened to be out. There was a great flurry of wings and six or seven shelduck rose from the marsh and flew out into the safety of the mud flats.

'Mrs Duffy sent you a piece of pie,' Joanna began, 'because . . .'

But Bob interrupted her. He said, 'I got a letter this morning.'

Something in his voice caught her attention. 'A letter?'

'From Bill. He wrote it yesterday. Sent it first class mail. At first I wondered whether I should tell you or not. But now, the way things have worked out, there doesn't seem to be any reason why you shouldn't read it.'

Joanna's heart went cold. 'Is it something dreadful?'

Bob laughed. 'Not dreadful. Funny, really, I suppose you'd call it.'

'Have you got the letter?'

In answer he reached into some back pocket and produced

a long envelope, rather crumpled. She recognised the Anderson trademark embossed on the back. She opened the envelope and took out the letter, and saw the familiar letter-head, and Mr William's writing saying 'My dear Bob'.

'You promise me it isn't anything dreadful?'

'I promise.'

Joanna read on.

By now you will have made the acquaintance of my friend Joanna, and I wish I could be at Whitebarns to witness your reactions to each other, but perhaps, as things are, it is better that I remain well out of the way.

You have so much in common. She is lonely and I think you are, too. She is shy, which is one of your failings. She also has a stubborn pride which is well-matched by your own. But these are on the negative side of the coin, and on the positive side are countless good things.

You haven't much time. For the first time in your life you may be faced with a hasty decision, the need to make up your mind what it is you want and go out and grab it. I have a feeling that you will, too, because my instincts for matching up, not only things, but people, tell me that you and Joanna are made for each other.

Good luck, and my love to you both,

Bill

She read the letter twice. She folded it and put it back in the envelope. Last night had seemed like a miracle, but it wasn't a miracle, it was something which had been coolly and thoughtfully contrived by Mr William, with his customary passion for perfection, and his infinite capacity for taking pains. As though they were two precious objects, made to complement each other, he had brought Joanna and Bob together, and they had fallen for his neat manipulation.

But had they? He had been right about Bob and Joanna, but he could have been wrong for no human being, no will-power could have fired that sudden passion, that instant recognition of each other as they stood beneath the trees of the dusky orchard and watched the new moon rise.

She said, 'He meant it to happen!'

'I know.' Bob was obviously more amused than annoyed. 'We've been manipulated. Do you object, my darling girl, to being manipulated?'

Part of her did, but it was so small a part as scarcely counted. And she had discovered that if you were safe and happy and loved, it became easy to laugh at yourself. Bob took her into the bear-hug of his arms and kissed her laughing, open mouth, and later on he said, 'When I see that brother of mine again, I shall either thank him or hit him,' but by then it was obvious that matters were totally out of Mr William's hands, and what-ever Bob chose to do could not count for a farthing, one way or the other.

Ghosts of the Past

Josephine Hanbury tilted her head back and forth, trying to get the flight information monitor in the airport arrivals hall into focus through her bi-focal spectacles. The plane was running fifteen minutes late. Probably a blessing that it was no more than that considering the Arctic weather conditions that had shrouded the entire country for the past week. She glanced around the area to see if there was a telephone booth near at hand, thinking that it might be best to call Douglas to say that the plane was going to be slightly delayed. Her husband had always been a stickler for punctuality, and would no doubt grumpily surmise that they were stuck in a snowdrift somewhere on the way back to the house if they were even a couple of minutes late.

A resigned smile crossed her face. Maybe on this occasion, his mind might be a little more preoccupied. He had only grunted her a farewell that morning as he sat watching the cricket on the kitchen television. It was being beamed, live from Australia, by way of that wretched satellite dish which now adorned the otherwise beautiful, wisteria-covered frontage of their house.

Through the milling crowd of passengers, she noticed a free telephone situated near to the Costa Coffee stall. She began to move towards it, taking one last fleeting look at the monitor to make sure that she was checking the correct flight, and immediately walked straight into an immoveable object. She reeled backwards, causing her spectacles to spin from her face and land with a clatter on the concrete floor.

She felt a steadying hand immediately grasp at her arm. 'I'm most terribly sorry,' a man's voice exclaimed. She did not look at him, but groggily fixed her blurred vision on the countless feet that passed within inches of her spectacles, feeling her face throb where she had come into contact with him.

'My spectacles,' she said weakly.

'Don't worry. I'll get them.'

The man bent stiffly forward to pick them up, leaning a hand on his knee to give himself support. He was dressed in a startlingly yellow duffel coat, the hood of which partially covered an unruly mass of white hair.

'There you are,' he said, holding out her spectacles to her. 'Might need a bit of straightening out, but I don't think there's any lasting damage done to them. I am sorry about that.'

Josephine smiled up at him. 'Please don't think that it was your fault. I just wasn't looking where I was going.' She made to take the spectacles from him, but for some reason he seemed reluctant to relinquish his grip on them.

'Good God!' he said quietly. 'Josephine?'

'I beg your pardon?'

'It is Josephine Hanbury, isn't it?'

There was something about the tone of his voice that she recognised. 'You have me at a disadvantage,' she said, letting out a nervous laugh. 'Could I have my spectacles, please?'

'I'm sorry,' he replied, immediately letting go of them.

She placed her spectacles back on her nose. Although one of the legs was so badly bent that she could only see through one of the lenses, it was enough to bring everything into focus. The long, angular face was all too familiar. She looked away, hoping that he might think that he had just made an embarrassing mistake.

'It is you, isn't it?' he asked again.

Josephine let out a sigh and smiled at the man, brushing away a wisp of grey hair that had been caught up on the useless leg of the spectacles. 'Yes, Humphrey. It is me.'

The man nodded slowly. 'I knew it was. You haven't changed at all.'

'In thirty years? You must be joking.'

'Well, I recognised you immediately.' He paused, smiling uneasily at her, and she realised by the flush that had risen to the cheeks of his craggy face that he too was embarrassed by their unscheduled meeting. 'So, what brings you here?'

'I'm meeting my daughter off the Heathrow plane.'

'That would be Helena, wouldn't it?'

Josephine swallowed hard. 'Yes. Well remembered. She comes up every month or so, just to make sure that we're both still live and kicking.'

'I see.' The man cast a glance around the arrivals hall. 'So how is Douglas?' Josephine detected a definite edge in the way that he asked the question.

'He's well. Still as . . .'

'Difficult as ever?' he interjected.

She looked directly at him. 'I wasn't going to say that.'

'I'm sorry. I shouldn't have said that.' He let out a deep breath and pushed his hands into the pockets of his duffel coat. 'Listen, do you want a cup of coffee or something? There's a Costa stall over there.'

'No thanks,' Josephine replied, almost too quickly. 'I mean, I don't think there's time. The plane will be landing soon.'

'Not for another five minutes, at least. I'm meeting my son off the same plane.'

Jack. That was the name of his son, but she wasn't going to admit to the knowledge.

'Touching base as well, is he?'

The man nodded. 'Exactly. He's been seconded to a company in Boston for two years, so he's coming up to say farewell to his old man.'

'That's a nice thought. Has he a family?'

'No. I'm afraid that he's married to his job, like so many of that generation nowadays. What about Helena?'

'Yes. She has two children.'

'Like yourself.'

'Yes, like myself.' This was all getting far too uncomfortable. She forced a friendly smile on to her face. 'Listen, Humphrey, I must go to the loo before the plane comes in. It really has been good to see you again.' She turned to go but he shot out a hand and grasped her elbow.

'Why did you never get in touch with me again, Josephine?'

She stared down at the hand. 'Please, Humphrey. I don't think that it would do any good dragging everything up again.'

'Well, you might not, but I would just like to know the answer. My understanding of the whole situation was that you were quite prepared to leave Douglas and come away with me. Is that not correct?'

'Humphrey, I . . .'

'Then suddenly I heard no more from you, and try as I might, I couldn't get in touch with you.'

Josephine sighed. 'That was because we'd said all that had needed to be said. It wasn't just "us" that had to be considered. We both had young children.'

'They would have survived.'

'And I was not prepared to risk that,' Josephine replied quickly, at the same time wrestling her arm free of his tightening grasp. 'Listen, Humphrey, I'm sorry that you obviously still feel so much hurt. I really am. But I can't say any more than that.' She noticed that there was movement at the arrivals gate, and glancing up at the monitor, saw with relief that the plane had landed earlier than expected. 'I have to go now. Goodbye.'

She turned and walked across the concourse floor to where the passengers from Heathrow would soon be arriving, desperately willing her daughter to be as speedy as she possibly could. When she did eventually appear ten minutes later, Josephine could feel her nerves still jangling from the encounter. Helena put her arms around her mother's neck and gave her a long hug. 'Hullo, Mum. How are you?'

'I'm well, my angel.'

'And Dad?'

Josephine pushed her gently away. 'As crotchety as ever, especially with this wretched weather. Let's just hope that England are winning the cricket, otherwise we'll both really be in for doom and gloom.' She surveyed her daughter's face. 'My word, darling, you look worn out. Come on, let's collect your case and get straight home.' She took hold of Helena's hand and started towards the already-moving carousel. Helena, however, held her back.

'I don't have a case, Mum.'

'Oh. Right. Travelling light this time, are you? Well, I suppose if you run out of clothes, there's bound to be some old ones still in your bedroom cupboard.'

Helena let out a sigh. 'Mum, can we go and have a cup of coffee?'

'What, now? Darling, if you wouldn't mind, I think that it would be better if we got home. The roads are . . .'

'Mum, I'm not coming home this time.'

Josephine frowned at her daughter. 'What do you mean you're not coming home? I don't understand. Are you going to be staying with someone else? If that's the case, why did you ask me to meet you?' She shook her head. 'Darling, I may be your mother, but I don't think that you should treat me as if I'm some sort of glorified taxi service. Do you know how long it took . . . ?'

'Mum, I'm not staying with anyone else, either. I'm actually catching the next plane back to London.'

'Catching the next plane? For what reason?' The puzzled frown on Josephine's face slid into a hardened stare of realisation. 'There's something wrong, Helena, isn't there? What's happened?'

'Listen, can we go and have a cup of coffee?'

'I don't want a cup of coffee,' she replied quite sharply. 'I want to know what's going on. There's not . . . anything wrong with the children, is there?'

'No, they're fine.'

Josephine let out a long puff of relief. 'Thank goodness for that!' She eyed her daughter. 'It's Philip, then, isn't it?' She noticed an immediate deflation in her daughter's posture. 'Oh, darling, I know what it is. He's lost his job. You did tell me there was a chance that . . .'

'Mum,' Helena cut in, 'Philip has not lost his job.' She bit at her lip. 'Listen, all the way up in the plane, I've been trying to come up with an easy way to break this to you, but, well, I couldn't – and I still can't.' She took in a deep breath, 'Philip and I have decided to split up.'

For the second time in so many minutes, Josephine felt as if she had just walked into an immoveable object. Only the impact from this one felt like the blow from a sledgehammer. 'What do you mean "split up"?'

'Just that. I can't put it any other way. Our marriage is finished. The only thing that we've both had success in doing over the past year is making each other's life a misery. And now, we simply cannot bear being in the same house together.'

Ghosts of the past, so recently brought to the fore, raged eerily in Josephine's head. 'But this is stupid! You can't leave him, Helena. You have your children to consider.'

Helena noticed that a number of her fellow passengers were beginning to find their conversation more engaging than watching for their suitcases on the carousel. 'Listen, Mum, can we please go and sit down somewhere?'

'No, we jolly well cannot. Listen, there is no way that you are going to walk out on your husband and your children.' She said it so loudly that those at the farthest length of the carousel now turned to look in their direction.

'All right,' Helena said quietly, keeping her eyes low but darting embarrassed glances around her. 'Keep your voice down.'

'Don't tell me to keep my voice down.'

She said it with such vehemence that Helena physically recoiled. 'I'm sorry.' She smiled at her mother, attempting some form of appeasement. 'Listen, Mum, the children will survive.'

'They will not survive, my girl. Now, I am having no more of this. Yes, you get on that next plane, but then you get straight back home and sort this whole thing out with Philip. The most important thing for you to realise right now is that it is never too late to salvage a marriage . . .'

'Mum, that is such a . . . I'm sorry, but it's such an *ignorant* thing to say. How could you ever know what Philip and I have been going through – what *harm* we've been doing to each other?'

Josephine stopped herself from shooting a glance across the concourse floor to where she had left the man. 'Believe me, my darling, I know.' She took hold of her daughter's hand. 'Listen, I know that you probably think that you feel miserable right now, but if you break up your family, you will experience . . .'

'But that's just it, Mum. I *don't* feel miserable now.' She let out a short laugh. 'For the first time in God knows how long, I feel wonderfully happy.'

Josephine let go of the hand and stared open-mouthed at her daughter. 'I don't understand.'

'I feel wonderfully happy, because I've met someone else, and he is everything that Philip has never, ever been. He is kind, understanding and he listens to me in such a way that makes me feel alive, intelligent and loved.' She paused. 'I'm not alone on this trip, Mum. I asked him to come up with me on the plane because I thought that if you met him, it would make it easier for you to understand what I'm doing, and why I'm doing it.' Helena reached out and took hold of her mother's inert hand and gave it what she hoped would be taken as a reassuring squeeze. 'He really is wonderful, Mum, and I love him very much.'

She turned away and scanned the arrivals hall, and Josephine watched as the momentary frown on her daughter's face was blown away by the pure radiation of excitement. She followed Helena's gaze to where, thirty paces away, a tall young man stood looking in their direction. He was dressed casually but smartly in an open-necked shirt and doublebreasted blazer, a look that was in total contrast to the white-haired man in the shambling yellow duffel coat who stood beside him.

Jonathan

In the same way that thousand-mile journeys start with the first step, so momentous events can begin to stir in the most humdrum and unexpected ways.

And yet they shouldn't have been unexpected, because the moment I woke up that morning, I had a feeling that something important was going to happen. For one thing a wind was rattling at the window of my bedroom sending the curtains billowing. When I got up to close the window, I saw the clouds, scudding across a June sky of deepest blue, and the sea was a marvellous dark aquamarine, speckled with white horses. A most exciting sort of day.

Below, in the farmyard, Mary's Brown Leghorn chickens pecked between the cobblestones for scraps of grain, and the wind caught their feathers and ruffled their knickerbockers, and their cackles and squawks sounded outraged.

The farm is called Polmeor and it belongs to my brother-in-law, Marcus Stevens. Marcus married my sister Mary ten years ago and they have seventy cows, sixteen pigs, three dogs, a flock of hens, a couple of evil-tempered geese and three children. The children, in their turn, have an aged donkey called Dearest, used as a pack horse to carry, in a couple of pannier baskets, bathing and picnic things down the cliffs to the beach. As likely as not, on the way home, one of the emptied panniers might also contain a leg-weary toddler on the climb up the valley from the cliff.

We were three sisters, all five years apart. Mary, and then Lally and then me. Our parents lived in Surrey, and in the summer holidays, we were taken either to the Lake District or Wales, or even, once or twice, to Spain. But after Mary married Marcus, Lally and I never wanted to go anywhere but Cornwall. Luckily the farmhouse is large and rambling, and my brother-in-law the most generous and hospitable of men.

And as for Mary, she welcomed us with open arms, for the three children came in quick succession, and extra and willing pairs of hands were more than welcome. You might think that hanging out lines of nappies, peeling great buckets of potatoes for the midday farm dinner, feeding hens and shelling peas isn't most people's idea of a summer holiday, but Polmeor is a magic place where even the most mundane tasks take on a joy of their own.

That day, Mary took the Land Rover into Porthkerris with a grocery list three pages long. I was left to put a load of sheets through the washing machine, tidy up the breakfast dishes, and make a shepherd's pie for lunch. I had everything done and the table laid, and was out in the garden pegging the sheets on the line, when Mary returned. I heard the car come into the farmyard, the pipe of a child's voice, a dog barking and doors slamming. I was on the last sheet when the house door opened and Mary came across the grass towards me, carrying two glasses of cider in her hands.

'What's this?' I asked. 'Drinking before lunch?'

'I need it, I'm exhausted.' She didn't look exhausted. She looked gorgeous, suntanned and blonde, like a Viking, I always thought. She had long hair in a pigtail now, and she wore faded corduroys and a coral pink T-shirt, and it was hard to believe that she was thirty and the mother of three children. I am dark-haired, and Lally is dark too, we are unmistakably related, but Mary is unique.

She flopped down on the worn grass and I sat beside her and took my glass of cider. All around us the sheets swung and snapped in the wind, there were three seagulls perched on the ridge of the barn roof, and the grass was starred with wide-eyed daisies.

Mary said, 'I've got news for you. I saw Mrs Crispin in the fruit shop – she was buying oranges. And she wants us all to go and have a drink with her tomorrow evening, because – wait for it – she's got Jonathan Locksley staying.'

It was just past noon and the sun was burning hot. I turned my head and looked at Mary, and we gazed into each other's eyes. My horrified astonishment must have shown in my face, because she said, ruefully. 'Yes, I know.'

'Did you say we'd go?'

'Of course I did. What else could I say? If we don't go the word will get around . . . that we're too guilty to show him our faces. And, after all, we have nothing to be guilty about – as Marcus continually tells me.'

'It's different for him. Lally isn't his sister.'

'That is what I continually tell him. But he just says that if Lally chose to elope with another man two weeks before she was due to marry Jonathan, then she's the one who should feel guilty.'

'I expect she did. For a little.'

'Yes, but it's difficult to sustain guilt, if you're living half a world away from your wicked deed, basking in the sunshine of Denver, Colorado, and with a well-heeled husband, to boot.' Mary lay back on the grass and closed her eyes. 'To boot. That's a marvellous expression, but I haven't the remotest idea what it means. Meantime you and I have to be charming to Jonathan and risk being cut dead.'

'He'd never be so unforgiving.'

'No, I don't suppose he would. He was a super man. I could never understand why Lally threw him over for Henry Hardacre.'

'We've never met Henry, so how can we know?'

'It wasn't as though he was particularly handsome. At least, he doesn't look it in his photographs. Why do Americans always have to wear such sincere spectacles?'

'Oh, Mary, *I* don't know.' It seemed to me that she was splitting hairs.

'Anyway I've said we'll go. We might as well get it over.'

I sighed. 'All right,' I said. 'I'll come.' And Mary had not an inkling of what it was going to cost me.

The midday meal was always a hefty affair at Polmeor, eaten at the big table in the kitchen. That day there were nine of us around the table: Mary and Marcus and me, three children – one in a highchair – Ernest the cowman, a young agricultural student who was helping out over the harvest, and Mrs Ernest who came in when she could to give Mary a hand with the housework. Conversation was general and Jonathan Locksley was not mentioned. After lunch had been cleared away and washed up, Mary led the children upstairs to wash the meal off them, dress them in clean clothes and take them to a party.

So I was left to my own devices. I went out into the garden, plucked my bikini and a faded towel off the washing line and set off, down the fields to the cliffs.

A stream runs through Marcus's land, gathering depth and momentum as it makes its way down from the moors. As it approaches the coast, it sinks down into a deep valley overgrown with hawthorn and knee deep in bracken, at that time lush with its new summer green. The path to the sea runs down this valley, hidden beneath the overhanging branches of the hawthorn. The air is sweet with the murmur of bees and bright with wild flowers that grow here like weeds; daffodils and primroses in springtime, and in summer, clumps of purple foxgloves as tall as a man.

The valley ends abruptly, just above the sea, the stream dropping down to the rocks in a miniature waterfall. I came out of the shelter of the trees and the wind pounced on me, as refreshing as a sluice of cold water.

The tide was out. The rocks, revealed, tumbled away beneath me, reaching long fingers out towards the creaming breakers, and, almost directly below me, Polmeor pool lay like a huge jewel in the grey granite, in places twenty feet deep or more.

There was a special rock above the pool where we always camped for picnics, marvellously sheltered from the sea wind and the right shape for sunbathing. I made my way now to this rock, dropped my bathing things beside me, and sat on its edge, my legs dangling. The sun was hot on my back, and it wasn't difficult to spirit myself back in time to that summer when Jonathan Locksley had come into our lives.

———

Mrs Christie, whom Mary had met this morning in the fruit shop, was his godmother. She was a splendid lady, large-bosomed and deep-voiced, a terror on committees, and famous for the fact that she was never seen without a hat.

She lived in a large white house, with a garden filled with palm trees and other semi-tropical vegetation. She also had a tennis court which, although it had fallen into a state of mild disrepair, she brought firmly back to use if the circumstances demanded it. Having her godson to stay was just such a circumstance, and we all dutifully went over one hot Sunday afternoon to play tennis.

I was fifteen, Lally was twenty and Mary, at twenty-five, already the mother of two little children. We were sisters, but we were very different. Mary was the domestic, home-making, maternal type. I was supposedly the intellectual. But Lally . . . Lally was the butterfly, the extrovert. No true beauty, she nevertheless had men falling in love with her from the moment she first opened her eyes. She might have been spoiled, but her sunny disposition and her ridiculous sense of humour somehow protected her. When she announced, at seventeen, that she wanted to go to drama school and become an actress, my parents made a few despairing noises, but it was only a token objection, and it was really no surprise to anybody when she got her own way.

She clowned and charmed and laughed her way through RADA, did a year with a provincial Rep, and then landed a small part in a new play which was opening in the West End.

It was terribly exciting. Our Lally was a real live actress, with her name on a poster in Shaftesbury Avenue.

But before this play went into rehearsal, Lally took a holiday. It was summer, and she and I came down to Polmeor. The summer of Mrs Christie's tennis party, the day we met Jonathan.

'My godson,' Mrs Christie had said over the telephone, and we had imagined some fresh-faced youth straight from school. 'He'll have rosy cheeks and spots and be wearing old cricket flannels, rather yellow,' Lally decided as we drove over to Penzance piled into the back of Marcus's car. 'And he'll say everything's *super*, and be dreadfully embarrassed when he makes a mess of his serve.'

We all giggled maliciously, as sisters will, but it was Jonathan who had the laugh on us, because not only was he quite old – at least mid-twenties – but immensely composed and charming. And he wore, not yellowed flannels, but a pair of honestly washed and worn jeans, and a whiter-than-white shirt, and his tennis was so good, even on his godmother's weedy old court, that he made the rest of us look like clumsy beginners.

But as well as all this, he was the nicest, funniest man any of us had met in years, and by the time we left he had promised to come out to Polmeor to see us. He was there the next evening, and we had supper in the garden, and then drove out along the cliff road to the local pub, where he said all the right things to the right people, and was even able to charm Ernest the cowman, who is a singularly uncharmable man.

After that, he was with us most of the time, arriving, unheralded, ready to turn his hand to any chore; playing cricket with the children; carrying the baby down to the rocks when we went on picnics. It was one of those summers when, in retrospect at least, the sun always seemed to be shining, the sea blue, the evenings drowsy with stored warmth. It was a time for love, and I fell, at fifteen, in love with Jonathan.

Nobody knew. Nobody guessed. I didn't even confide in Mary, for Mary was married to Marcus, and the slightest hint to him would have brought on a spate of unmerciful teasing. So I kept my love to myself, a secret to be dreamed about.

It wasn't as drastic a situation as it sounds. Jonathan was too old, too remote, too marvellous for my infatuation to become anything more than just that. To him, I was simply the little sister. I never thought of him and Lally. He was obviously enchanted by her, but everybody was enchanted by her.

Then one afternoon he and Lally and I took Henrietta, Mary's eldest child, down to swim in Polmeor pool. Up at the farm it had been baking hot, but by the sea the breeze was cool and the waters of the pool as icy as ever. Henrietta was too little to swim in the deep waters – she was only three at that time – so I swam first and then took her hand and led her over the rocks to another shallow pool and went back to fetch her bucket.

But I never got the bucket, because I saw Lally and Jonathan first. They never saw me. They sat together, on the rock by the Polmeor pool. Lally between Jonathan's tanned knees, her back cradled against his chest. His arms were around her, his chin resting on the top of her head. The soft murmur of their contented voices reached me over the gentle buffet of the breeze.

That was all. But there was about them a togetherness, as though love had ringed and enclosed them, shutting them away from the rest of the world. I saw Lally's long tanned legs, her head against his shoulder. I saw him smile at something she said.

A black, shaming jealousy clawed at my heart. Like a rage, it engulfed and left me shivering. The little red bucket lay beside them, but I backed away, out of sight.

I closed my eyes and took a deep breath and told myself firmly how nice, how wonderful, they were in love, he would probably marry her, he would become my brother-in-law.

I told myself, in my mother's voice, that I would get over it. Everybody had a first love, and it would never be the same. I was, after all, only fifteen. I told myself that there were better fish in the sea than ever came out of it. I told myself . . .

I was crying. But crying wasn't any good, because I had to get back to Henrietta before she drowned herself or came searching for me.

———•◦•———

And so Lally went back to London, not only a budding actress with a part in a West End play, but engaged to Jonathan Locksley as well. It was all very convenient because he was working in London; he had a flat there, and he used to come down to my parents' house at weekends. My mother adored him, and my father thought he was a good fellow and everything was perfect.

The invitations for the wedding went out, my mother made lists, my father wrote cheques, and the presents came rolling in. I was going to be a bridesmaid, and my mother got me the prettiest dress I had ever seen.

I don't quite know how Lally met Henry Hardacre, but I suspect he saw the play in London one night, and came round to her dressing-room afterwards with a bunch of flowers, or something like that. Americans are always very good about bringing bunches of flowers. Anyway, she let him take her out for dinner, and the next night she phoned Jonathan to say that she had a headache and she was going to bed early, but instead she went out with Henry Hardacre.

The next Sunday she came home for the day, and we all noticed how tired and pale and distraite she seemed, but I put it down to the business of having to act every night and my mother said it was pre-wedding nerves. Lally went back to

London and none of us gave her obvious depression another serious thought. We just went on opening parcels and ringing up the man about the marquee and trying to decide how much wine we were going to need.

But in the end we didn't need any wine, because the next week Lally left the play, another girl took over her part, and she and Henry Hardacre were married in London by special licence. The first we knew of it was a telegram we received from Heathrow airport, and by the time we got it, she was already over the Atlantic and on her way to her new life in Denver, Colorado.

From there she wrote a long, loving and apologetic letter, which made it impossible for us not to understand and forgive her. My parents behaved quite perfectly. After the first appalling shock, a few tears (from my mother) and a few unprintable expletives (from my father) they gathered themselves together and set about unscrambling the wedding preparations.

This was all bad enough, but nothing was as bad as the inevitable session with Jonathan. He came down to see us the day after Lally disappeared. She had written him a letter which had been waiting for him on his desk when he got to the office that morning. He had a long talk with my parents (I pretended to be ironing in the kitchen, and I could hear their voices going on and on from the other room while I made a bungling mess of one of my father's shirts).

When it was time for him to go, my mother called to me and I went out into the hall to say goodbye. He was composed as ever, but his face had a pallor like white blotting paper, and somehow I couldn't look into his eyes. That was the last time I saw him.

Ever since the debacle of the wedding that never took place, I had been sustaining myself with clichés. Time is a great healer. Water flows under the bridge. Tastes change, even in men. The person you love at fifteen is not necessarily the person you love at twenty. But still I remembered him. His tall, erect and slender shape, his voice, his eyes, filled with laughter.

'He'll be over thirty by now,' Mary worked out, as we drove over the moor in a golden evening to have drinks with Mrs Christie.

'An old, old man,' said Marcus, who was nearing forty.

'I think,' said Mary, 'I'd feel better about it all if only he'd married. But he's still footloose and fancy free. I wonder why? He was so wildly attractive.'

'Perhaps he was more in love with Lally than any of you realised.'

'Or perhaps,' suggested Mary brightly, 'he's turned all twisted and bitter.'

Marcus groaned. 'Give the man a chance.'

We were the last to arrive at the party. There we found many cars parked on the gravel sweep outside Mrs Christie's house, and the three French windows of the drawing-room were open to the sloping lawns and some of her guests had already found their way out there to admire her garden, smell the roses, look at the view.

We went into the house and through the hall and the noise

of concentrated conversation came out and hit us. I always hate going into a crowded room, there is something quite terrifying about it, but someone gave me a drink at the door, and Marcus gave me a shove from behind, and the next moment Mrs Christie was bearing down on us, resplendent in her best gaberdine, and wearing – yes, wearing her hat: a sort of velvet turban.

'Oh, my dears, how nice to see you. I was afraid you weren't going to be able to come. What a beautiful evening, you simply mustn't go home without taking a look at my philadelphus, it's quite perfect. Now, who do you know? You probably know everybody . . .'

———

He was here, somewhere in this room full of people. A prickling sensation down the left side of my face warned me of his presence. I have always been very sensitive to other people's stares. I turned my head slowly, and, across the room, across a haze of cigarette smoke and a sea of chattering heads, our eyes met.

They were very dark and deepset eyes, and his face was thinner and his hair a little longer than I remembered. But otherwise he was exactly the same. And so was I, because all those clichés with which I had been comforting myself over the years evaporated into thin air, and there I was, in love with Jonathan all over again.

He didn't smile. I went cold, thinking that perhaps he was going to turn away from me and cut me dead, but after a long moment, he excused himself to the woman standing next to him and politely edged his way through the throng. When at last he reached my side, he took my hand in his, and I thought he was going to kiss me, but he only said my name.

Its sound was sweet on my ears. I said, 'Hello, Jonathan.'

He shook his head, a man confused by his own astonishment. 'Why did I imagine you were going to stay a little girl for ever? My godmother told me she'd asked you and Mary and Marcus, and I had a mental picture of you just the way you used to be. And here you are, all grown up and looking like . . .' His voice tailed away.

With more courage than I ever suspected I was capable of, I finished the sentence for him: 'Looking like Lally.'

I had said her name, and it was like a door opening between us. Jonathan hesitated, and then he began to smile. 'Yes. Lally. I suppose that is what I meant. How is she?' I opened my mouth to tell him, but he stopped me. 'No, don't tell me here, I can't hear myself think. Come on, we'll go out into the garden.'

He was still holding my hand, and he turned and led me back across the room and out through the French windows into the blessed open air. A few elderly pieces of garden furniture had been arranged around the lawn, but these were already occupied by older guests who didn't relish standing, so Jonathan and I went a little way off, and he took off his jacket in a most chivalrous manner and spread it on the grass and we sat on that.

'Now tell me. How is Lally?'

'Happy.'

'It was a brave thing she did. It must have taken a lot of courage. Has she ever been home?'

'No. She's always talking about making a visit, but she hasn't yet. Perhaps next year, before she starts a family.'

'And how are you all? And your parents?'

'Very well. They're in Scotland just now, playing golf.'

'I . . .' He looked down into his glass. 'I wanted to come and see them again, after Lally went off like that. I wanted to keep in touch with you all. I didn't want to lose you. But I got sent abroad, and when I came back to London last year, I was afraid I'd just be opening up old wounds if I got in touch with you again. I was so sorry for your mother and father. They behaved so splendidly, and they were very kind to me. It was a gruesome thing to happen to them.'

'It was a pretty gruesome thing to happen to you, too.'

'It was probably for the best.' He looked into my face. 'I'm glad it's worked out for Lally.'

'I wish you'd got married . . .' I started, and then stopped, because of course this was a total lie and I didn't wish he'd married at all. 'I mean, perhaps then we wouldn't feel that your life was totally ruined.'

He began to laugh. 'Totally ruined,' he told me. 'Can't you see, after all these years of despair, I've become a shambling wreck.' And I laughed too, because no man had ever looked less of a shambling wreck. 'Don't worry, I was far too busy, and anyway, I never met anybody I wanted to marry. And now don't let's talk about me any more. I want to hear all about you. What's happening to you?'

'I'm at university.'

'It figures, as they say. You were always the bright one of the family. What are you reading?'

'Modern languages.'

'And you're spending the vacation with Mary and Marcus?'

'Right. She's got three children now, and Henrietta's nearly eight. Do you remember Henrietta?'

'I remember Henrietta, and Dearest the donkey. And I remember being sent out into the garden to dig up potatoes, and picnics at Polmeor pool.'

'I was down there yesterday. The tide was out and the pool was as deep and blue and cold as ever. Nothing's changed.'

He said, 'Yes, it has. Everything's changed. Nothing ever stays the same. We all grow older, we're born, we die. Henrietta is eight. Lally is far away. The pattern constantly changes.'

His words made me feel wise and old. Sad and happy at the same time. I said, 'If I asked you, would you come back to Polmeor and see us all? Would you come, or would it be too full of memories?'

'I'd come. I'd have come days ago, only I thought it might embarrass you all.'

'Oh, Jonathan, how stupid we all are! Mary and I didn't really want to come here this evening because we thought it was going to be so uncomfortable and difficult . . . seeing you again, I mean.'

'And is it?'

I very nearly kissed him. I said, 'No.'

'In that case, let's pretend we've only just met each other, for the first time. Let's pretend that I've taken a fancy to you, and I'm going to ask you to come out to dinner with me. We'll find some crafty nook hung about with lobster pots and we'll eat crabs or clotted cream or whatever happens to be on the menu. Would you like that?'

Someone called my name. We looked up and saw Mary and Marcus coming across the twilit lawn towards us. And a curious thing happened. It was like watching a film when the projector suddenly breaks, and you are left watching a single frame, a picture frozen to stillness. That instant was crystallised, for me, forever; the expression on Mary's face when she saw us sitting together, the blue dusk of the garden, the scent in the air of orange blossoms; the long lighted windows of the old house. And Jonathan.

My love. My only love.

It was over in a second. Mary was saying, 'We've been looking everywhere for you,' and Jonathan stood up to greet her. He took her in his arms and kissed her as though indeed she were his sister. And Mary hugged him back and said, 'Oh, Jonathan, how wonderful to see you again.'

I remembered then how the day had started, with the wind blowing, and the bright sunshine, and Mary coming across the garden at Polmeor to tell me that Jonathan was back, and we had both been filled with foreboding.

But now . . . Now I felt that anything could happen. Thousand-mile journeys do begin with the first step. Jonathan took my hand and pulled me to my feet, and I had visions of us, hand-in-hand, plodding along down the years with rucksacks on our backs.

I began to laugh. He asked me why I was laughing, but I didn't tell him. But perhaps, one day, I will.

The Key

A long time ago, the village had slept, remote and rural, at the foot of the Cotswolds, but as main roads stretched out from London, and more and more city people sought the serenity of the country, it had gradually changed.

The family grocer was taken over by a national supermarket, and the butcher's premises were bought out by an antique dealer. As well, there was now a little dress shop, inordinately expensive, and a couple of estate agents.

On a Saturday morning in June, a car turned the corner at the foot of the long street, and made its way slowly up the gentle incline, shaded by lofty trees. At the wheel was a girl, slender, dark-haired, quite young; she had driven that morning from London. Now, as she drove, she leaned forward to scan the names above the shop fronts, and when she saw the estate agents' office, she drew into the road side, parked carefully, and turned off the engine.

She got out of the car, crossed the pavement and let herself in through the glassed door, to find herself in a modern office where a young man sat behind a desk.

He smiled, ready and willing to help this tall, pretty young woman, and got to his feet.

'Good morning.'

'Good morning. I'm sorry to bother you, but I'm looking for a house. It's called Stenton, and it's in this village . . .'

The young man did not wait for more. 'Of course,' he said at once. 'You want to go and see the house.'

'Yes, but . . .'

The young man, trained in salesmanship, over-rode this mild hesitation. 'Do we have your name?'

'It's Ruth Conway, but I haven't phoned or anything, so you won't have any record.'

'I see.' He smiled again. 'What I call an impulse viewing. You won't be disappointed, I'm sure. It's a charming little house and fully furnished.'

'It's . . .' she hesitated again, searching for the right words. 'You said it was a *little* house?'

'Used to be part of a stable complex.'

'But there's a big house, too?'

'That's a ruin now. It burned down about three years ago. Just after the old lady, who had lived there all her life, died.'

'But – how? Why?'

'An electrical fault, and because the house was empty at the time there was no one to raise the alarm. The first the village knew of the tragedy was seeing the flames leaping from the roof. And, of course, by then it was too late. It was a very old house; Elizabethan, you know, and panelled throughout. It went up like tinder.'

———

There was a pause while Ruth Conway digested this information. Then she said, 'I didn't know.'

'How could you?'

Now he looked at her more closely. She was wearing a pleated skirt and a navy-blue sweater. Her legs were beautiful, very long and slender, and around her neck – and this was almost more eye-catching than the legs – was a gold chain. From this hung a heavy round medallion, depicting the embossed head of a man. It looked, to the assessing eye of the young agent, both old and genuine. He wondered how she had come by such a thing.

She said, 'The other house – the little one that's for sale—'

'For rent,' he corrected her quickly.

'Would I be able to see it?'

'Yes, I think so. The only thing is –' he pushed back a starched cuff, consulted a silver watch – 'I have a client coming in at any moment, so I wouldn't be able to come with you.'

'Could I go by myself?'

He looked surprised and a little put out. 'I – I should think so. I'll find out. If you'll just wait for a moment, I'll make a phone call.'

He took himself off into some back office to make the necessary phone call, although there was a perfectly good telephone right there on the desk. Ruth waited. Presently he reappeared, all smiles.

'That'll be all right. Here we are.' He opened a drawer and produced a key with a chain and a little label. She took it from him, and stood with it in the palm of her hand, her head bent, her face hidden from him by that fall of heavy dark hair. 'Now,' He said, 'do you know how to find the house?'

She raised her head. 'I've no idea.'

'Never been here before?'

'No.'

'Excuse my asking, but you're an Australian, aren't you?'

'Yes, I am. My father has a sheep station about fifty miles from Melbourne.'

'Is this your first visit to Britain?'

'Yes.'

'Enjoying it?'

'Yes. Very much.'

The young man went to open the door and together they stepped out into the sunny flower-scented afternoon.

'Up the street,' he told her. 'Past that last big house and then take the small lane to the right. That leads to the gates of Stenton. You go up the drive as far as the house, and you'll see the stables on your left.'

'You've been very helpful. I'll bring the key back.'

'Yes, please. And if I'm not here and the office is locked, then just drop it through the letter-box. And if you're interested in the house, perhaps you could give me a telephone call later on in the afternoon. I don't shut up shop until five. Here . . .' He felt in some inner pocket. 'My card.'

She took the card, and read his name and telephone number. He was called, she saw, W. T. Redward.

Back behind the wheel of her car, heading up the street in the direction he had indicated she had time to feel a little guilty about W. T. Redward as one must about any person one had deceived, however harmlessly.

But there were other and more absorbing things to occupy her mind, and the guilt lasted only for an instant. She reached the turning and found herself in a narrow lane which curved away between grassy banks and an avenue of beeches. As she came around the curve, an immense pair of gateposts reared up before her, and she knew then that she had come to Stenton.

The driveway was short, and almost at once the sad ruin came into view, set back beyond a stretch of rough grass which must once have been a lawn of velvet smoothness. The drive divided and circled this, to meet again in a gravelled carriage sweep, but here again weeds grew rampant, and brambles twined with the ancient unpruned roses which still clung to the broken walls of the house.

She stopped the car and got out. The place had an air of desolation, of quiet, as though caught in a vacuum of silence and decay.

***

She looked at the roofless, eyeless wreck of the old house and felt sad. Here families had lived, children had played, aproned maids had carried tea-trays; babies had been born, old men had died. Here had laughed young girls in white muslin, dressed for their first parties, with the house filled with music.

She began to walk across the gravel, her footsteps alarmingly loud on the loose stones. It had rambled, this old house. One wing had been razed to the ground, but the centre section still stood as tall as the first floor, with the ornate doorway set beneath a giant slab of golden Cotswold stone. The door was oak, and ajar. Cautiously, Ruth went forward and pushed it gently inwards.

It moved with a creak. Beyond lay what had once been the hallway, but the floor was broken and charred, exposing great voids of black space, so there could be no question of going farther. But the great stone fireplace still stood, and the remains of an enormous staircase.

She was filled with frustration. Having come so far, she could go no farther. The place was a death trap. After a little she backed away, pulling the door shut behind her. She turned, and saw the man walking across the grass towards her.

His hair was dark and curly and a black Labrador ran at his heels. As Ruth stepped out from under the doorway the Labrador barked, but the man quietened him with a movement of his hand.

'It's dangerous,' he told her. 'You mustn't go in. I put up a Keep Out sign, but the boys from the village must have knocked it down.' He had a thin face, dark eyes and an unmistakable air of distinction.

'Have you come to see the stable house? You're Miss – Conway, I think Mr Redward said.'

'Yes. Ruth Conway. Was it you he telephoned?'

'Yes. I'm Gavin Armitage.'

'Do you own all this?'

'Yes.' He smiled then, wryly, but it changed his whole rather forbidding appearance. 'What remains of it.'

'I can't bear it.' She turned back to look at the sad, scarred face of the old house. 'It must have been so beautiful.'

'It was.'

'Mr Redward told me it burned down after the last owner died.'

'Yes.' He added, as though it were of no consequence, 'She was my grandmother. She loved the house almost more than life itself. She'd been born here and she was married from the house, and she had all her children here, and she lived here as a widow, and finally died, quite peacefully, in her own bedroom.'

'Was she an only child?' Ruth prompted.

'No. She had a brother and a sister. The brother was killed in the First World War, and the sister eloped with the gardener's boy and was never heard of again. So when my grandmother married, her father made Stenton over to them. But it was always her house. From beginning to end, it was her house.'

'She must have been a lady of some means to have kept a place this size going.'

'She didn't have means so much as determination. After she was widowed, she decided that nothing would make her give up the house, so she opened it to the public. Summer Saturdays and Sundays you could scarcely move for visitors, and my grandmother was always there, either showing people around, or brewing up another urn of tea, or talking flowers to any person who showed the slightest interest.'

'She sounds fun.'

'She was.'

'And now it all belongs to you?'

'Yes. My father's still alive, but he lives and works in London. For some reason Stenton never meant that much to him. But my grandmother knew that I loved it just as much as she did. She wanted me to live here. But the old house had other ideas. It was uncanny. As though it didn't want anyone but her to live here . . .' His voice died away. And then, with a smile that was both apologetic and faintly embarrassed: 'Don't know why I'm talking so much. You've come to see the stable house, not to have your time wasted.'

'It's not wasting time, I assure you. Go on telling me. Where do you live?'

'That was no problem. Stenton isn't just a house, it's an estate, with a farm. I live in the farmhouse and try to make the land pay its way. It's a struggle. But that's why I want to let the stable house.'

———•◦•———

She said nothing to this. After a little, in a changed tone of voice he said, 'You know you sound like an Australian . . .'

'That's because I am one.'

'Why should you want to rent a house in the Cotswolds?' She shrugged. 'I just do.'

'Come along then. I'll take you to see it.'

She followed him and the dog around the side of the charred walls to where, within an old stable-yard wall, a cottage had been newly converted. The windows were bright, the roof re-tiled, the front door painted a cheerful blue.

'Have you got the key?'

Ruth took it from her pocket and gave it to him. He opened the door, and she followed him inside.

'That's the sitting-room, and then beyond it the kitchen-dining room. This faces east, so you'll get all the morning sun. And there's a utility room in here . . .' He opened a door, and they peered inside. 'Clothes washer and a dryer. And upstairs – ' she followed his long legs up a steep stairway, carpeted in cherry red – 'there are three bedrooms, two with basins, and a bathroom, and an airing cupboard.'

Downstairs again, they returned to the sitting-room. 'There's central heating, of course, but an open fire as well. If you like, I can sell you logs from my saw-mill . . .'

'What a farce this is!' he remarked. 'You're not interested in renting this place, are you?'

She shook her head. 'I got talked into coming by W. T. Redward.'

'That's no answer. There's something fishy going on.'

'What makes you say that?'

'Finding you nosing around the ruins of the house. And this – I noticed it at once.' And he reached out a hand and took up the heavy gold medallion, holding it in his palm.

She looked back into his face. His dark eyes were watchful.

'What does that tell you?'

'My grandmother had the twin of it. I have it now. Mine is the head of a woman. I think they must have been struck as a love token, or a seal of engagement. They're very old and very valuable. My great-grandfather brought them back from Italy, and gave one to each of his daughters as an eighteenth birthday present. So this one belonged to . . .'

151

'Amy,' said Ruth. 'The one who eloped with the gardener's boy and was never heard of again. *My* grandmother.'

'What became of her?'

'They sailed to Australia, and they married. The gardener's boy was my grandfather.'

'Did they make a success of their life together?'

'Very much so. Although he was a man of humble birth and, I suppose, little formal education, he was a hard worker and he had a sort of natural astuteness. In time he bought land, raised sheep, built a house. That grew into the sheep station where I was brought up. My father still runs the place. It's called Turramoolagong.'

'Turramoolagong,' he repeated, and began to laugh.

'What's so funny?'

'I never realised I had a second cousin called Ruth Conway living in a place called Turramoolagong. Life is full of surprises.'

'Second cousins? I suppose we are.'

'How long have you been in this country?'

'Just six months. My grandmother died and left me a little money. She said in her will it was to pay my fare back home, as she resolutely called England all her life. And I'd trained as a nurse, working mostly with children, so living in London I can earn my keep, and more, being a nanny. I've a good job right now, for three months – this is just my weekend off – but when this job is finished I hope I'll have saved enough to get around and see a bit of the country.'

'But why Stenton? Why did you come to Stenton?'

'Oh, Gavin . . .' His name came out quite naturally, as

though she had been using it for years. 'If only you knew how much I know about the place. Granny used to talk on and on about how it used to be when she was a girl, and I would listen forever, hearing about the parties and the picnics and the Christmases, with a tree in the hall so tall that it reached to the third landing. I knew how the house looked, every brick and stone of it, long before I drove the car through the gates. That is why I wanted to go in, and be there. Walking through the rooms, even if they were ruined and charred and windowless. But of course I couldn't even do that.'

'I'm sorry.'

'For what?'

'That the house, like the two old ladies, is dead.'

———·•·———

All this time, as they talked, he had been holding the medallion. Now he let it go, and she felt its weight drop against her breast. 'So what happens now?' he asked.

Ruth shrugged. 'I return the key and drive back to London.'

'But you've got a weekend off. Don't you want to stay? Stay,' he pressed her. 'Not in a pub or an hotel, but with me. I've masses of space and a guest room – also a housekeeper.'

'What will your wife say when I turn up?'

'Blessed girl, I haven't got a wife.'

'I'd like to stay,' she said simply. 'I think we've got a lot to talk about.'

'Yes, I think we have. And I want to show you the twin to

your medallion,' he said. 'And we can pore over old photograph albums and read old diaries and wallow in nostalgia.'

He then leaned forward and set a kiss upon her mouth, a swift and unpassionate kiss that was more a greeting than a gesture of affection.

In Ruth's car, with Gavin behind the wheel, and the black Labrador sitting up in the back seat like a person of much importance, they drove back to the village and the estate agents' office. Ruth got out of the car and crossed the pavement to try the door. It was, however, locked. W. T. Redward had not yet returned. She took the key out of her pocket and . . .

For a moment she hesitated, thoughtful, standing there with the key in the palm of her hand. A very ordinary little latchkey, opening the door to an ordinary house which she had never even wanted to see. But it had opened other doors as well, perhaps changing the whole course of her life. A door to the past. A door to the future. Who could tell?

She smiled, and dropped the key through the letter-box, and then turned and went back to where he waited for her. Her second cousin. Her new friend. Gavin.

A Fork in the Road

Maggie was late. This was nothing unusual, and in the two years that he had known her, Alistair had spent more time than he cared to contemplate waiting for her to show up. But this was going to be a special evening – an expensive evening – and he had taken some trouble with his own appearance: buttoned on a new shirt, shined his shoes, carefully chosen a tie. After all this effort, it was faintly galling to find himself, yet again, sitting on a bar stool, waiting for Maggie.

The Candide was his favourite restaurant – exactly the right size, the right lighting, the right smells. He thought, *This is one of the places I shall miss if I leave London. There'll be nothing remotely like this in the frozen North.*

There were other things he'd miss. The sounds of London: tugs hooting on the river and the cry of wheeling gulls. The sights: the evening skies and the Tate Gallery. And most of all, the sensation of being at the heart of things, with friends, and with Maggie . . .

'Darling, I'm late, I'm late, but here I am . . .'

And there she was, tall as a beanpole, bearing down on him, laden with bags. Her milk-pale hair was scraped back from her face and pinned into a tiny bun. She wore dark glasses, and tottered slightly as she approached him, as though she had run six miles in order to finally arrive at his side.

He relieved her of her bags, and she climbed on to the stool beside him, then went into a long and familiar string of excuses.

'I haven't even been home to change, and you're looking so handsome. Is that a new shirt? Anyway, I've been with Sebastian all day, closeted in his beastly studio.'

Alistair smiled. Sebastian was the best-known fashion photographer in the country, and Maggie was his favourite model, yet they never seemed to do anything but row.

'Anyway . . .' She took off her glasses and he was confronted by her amazing eyes, made enormous by smudges of kohl. 'Here I am, and what's the celebration?'

'No celebration.'

'But darling, there has to be. Nobody ever comes here unless they're celebrating. Or else drowning horrible sorrows. It's far too expensive.'

'I don't think it's either.'

'But it is something.' Despite her dotty mannerisms, Maggie was no fool.

'Yes, I'll tell you over dinner.'

———◦✦◦———

He duly told her. 'I've been offered a new job. In Edinburgh. Barkers has decided to open a new property office up there. There's a great market in the area with all these oilmen in from all over the world.'

'But why you? What does Barkers want you to do?'

'Start it up. Run it. I haven't given them an answer yet.'

'Do you want to go?'

'I don't know.'

'Is this why you brought me here tonight? To tell me this?'

'I have to talk about it with someone. And you seemed the obvious person.'

She eyed him thoughtfully. 'Am I involved?'

He found that he had no answer. She had been part of his life for two years now. He was very fond of her. She made him laugh. She was part of London, one of many things he did not want to leave. He didn't even know whether he could bear to live without her.

He said, 'You wouldn't want to come to Scotland.'

'Are you asking me, or stating a fact?'

'Just feeling my way.'

'If you're asking me, the answer is no. I couldn't work away from London. I couldn't *live* away from London.'

'And I'm not that important to you anyway.'

'Darling, of course you're important.'

He hesitated, then took a sip of wine. 'If I asked you to marry me, would you?'

They stared at each other in astonishment, as though it was not Alistair who had said these words, but some other person.

'Who's talking of getting married?' she asked.

'Pretend it's hypothetical. Would you?'

'Not if it meant living away from London. I'd go mad.'

'How can you be sure when you've never been to the place?'

'I have been to Edinburgh. I nearly froze to death.'

'It's a great place. I spent four years there at university.'

'I can't imagine it.' She gazed at him, screwing up her eyes.

'But then I can! You, all wound up in mufflers and tweed, making instant coffee in some freezing attic.'

'Wrong. I lived with a delightful family who took me to their bosoms as though I were their son.'

She laughed suddenly. One of Maggie's most endearing traits was her sense of humour, which bubbled up when least expected. 'Can you speak with an Edinburgh accent?'

He said, 'Ay had an Ant Mod once, but she dayed,' and then they were both laughing and didn't talk about the new job or Edinburgh any more.

He took her to her flat, then walked home along the river. He was not sure whether he was disappointed or relieved by the evening. He knew only that he was twenty-eight, that he had come to a fork in the road, and that he didn't know which way to go.

The prospect of leaving Maggie left an emptiness that he could not imagine filling. He had asked her to marry him on a whim, and she had given him no sort of answer. Except that she wasn't going to consider moving North. But on the other hand, did he love her enough to give up the new appointment and stay in London? He realised that he didn't have the answer. All at once he was angry at himself for being so ineffectual. He stuffed his hands in his pockets and quickened his pace. Ten minutes later he was back in his own flat, dialling his boss's number.

Two days later he was in Edinburgh, casing the market, getting the feel of the place again. It was February and bitterly cold. He had forgotten the winds, whistling up the wide streets from the north. He had forgotten the immensity of the sky, the towering hulk of the castle, the stones of houses gleaming in the cold, pure light. All of it was familiar, and yet new.

By five o'clock, he was back in his hotel room, putting through a call to his office. When the business end of their call was through, his boss said, 'That sounds good, Alistair. Worth going ahead.'

'I'll get it all written down before I come back.'

'When will that be?'

'I'll drive home tomorrow.'

'Don't rush it. Enjoy yourself while you're there.'

Alistair grinned. 'I'll do that, I'm having dinner tonight with the family I lived with when I was up here at university.'

When they had hung up, he sat and made a few notes for his report, then changed and went downstairs to wait for Janey. 'I'll come and fetch you,' she had said, insisting that the new one-way streets would confuse him. So he had let himself be persuaded and now sat and watched the revolving door and wondered if he would recognise her.

When she came, she looked exactly the same. They met in the middle of the lobby and hugged. Six years had passed, and she had married and had two children, but all this seemed to have had no effect at all upon her appearance.

'Oh,' she said, looking at him. 'You haven't changed a bit. What a relief.'

'Nor have you. You look exactly the same.'

She had dark hair and bright blue eyes and a smile that warmed the heart. 'I can't tell you how excited we all are. Mother's killed a fatted calf – well, actually plucked a brace of pheasants – and Dad's promised to try not to be caught up at the hospital. Oh, let's go . . .' She shook his arm. 'We haven't any time to waste.'

In the car, she brought him up to date on the family. 'We split the house in three. It got far too expensive to keep warm, so we had a hideous year with builders, and now it's three flats. George and I and the children live on the top floor, and then Mother and Dad and Henrietta live in the middle and we've let out the basement.'

'I've never met your husband.'

'No, you haven't, have you? He's terribly nice, and the children are nice, too, most of the time, but they'll probably be in bed by the time we get back, so you won't have to think up things to say about them.'

'And your father?'

'He's working harder than ever. He keeps threatening to retire, but we all pray he won't, because goodness knows what he'd do to himself without his precious hospital. And my mother's opened a shop!'

'And Douglas?'

'Brother Douglas is in the Army, so you won't see him, I'm afraid. But Henrietta's still at home, and going to art school. She suddenly developed a flair for design.'

Alistair shook his head in disbelief. He remembered

162

Henrietta with long, pale plaits of hair and stick-thin legs emerging from her school tunic.

'And Wimpy?'

Wimpy had been Henrietta's dog.

'Poor Wimpy had to be put down. But Henrietta got another dog . . .'

Janey chattered on, and he felt comfortable and suddenly happy, sitting beside her, listening to her voice. He had always been fond of her – never in love, but always loving. They had become close in those years when they were living, cheek-by-jowl, in the same house. It was like having the very closest sort of sister except that they never quarrelled.

'. . . he's called Charles, but he's got no breeding whatsoever.' He realised that she was still talking about the dog. 'But tell me about you.'

So he told her, very briefly, ending by explaining the purpose of his visit. Janey was immediately excited.

'I can't think that it wouldn't be a success. And it'd be super if you came back to run it.'

'Now, hold on, I haven't said I'm going to yet. I don't know if I want to leave London.'

'But it would be a challenge. You always used to be a great one for challenges.'

He knew that was true. But somehow he couldn't explain to Janey how things had changed, how he found himself in a dilemma he seemed incapable of resolving. He was on the point of telling her about Maggie, but she suddenly said, 'Nearly there,' and he realised that they were now in the familiar crescent of tall Georgian houses. He saw the wide flight of steps leading up to the fan-lighted front door and the facade of the handsome stone house.

They got out of the car, and Janey led the way. She opened the door, and a woolly mass of dog came to greet them, and behind him, with her arms outspread in welcome, Mrs Randall.

The house had been converted, but nothing could change the warmth that pervaded it. The brightness of the fire, the overflow of books, the profusion of plants and flowers, family photographs, and unfinished knitting. The smells of delectable cooking, and polish and wood smoke. And Mrs Randall herself, white hair like an aureole about her cheerful face, lipstick slightly askew, laughing with excitement.

'Oh, Alistair, isn't this the most thrilling thing? And you look just the same. Take off your coat, come along in, it's such a cold night.'

She led him in, literally pulling him by the arm. And there, in the sitting room, was Dr Randall, still looking as if he had bought his suit at a rummage sale; and another man, younger and bespectacled, who was introduced as Janey's husband, George. And then they all had a drink and were sitting down, deep in the sagging armchairs, out of which, Alistair knew from experience, it was almost impossible to heave oneself.

What made it even more impossible was that the dog, Charles, who was not small, decided that Alistair's knee was infinitely preferable to his own lumpy cushion on the hearth rug, and leaped into Alistair's lap where he settled himself in heavy comfort.

They were on their second drink and still talking when the door opened. He had forgotten about Henrietta, but all at once, Mrs Randall stopped talking in midstream, looked toward the door and said, 'Darling!'

'I'm sorry I'm late.'

The dog leaped from Alistair's knee and went to greet her. She shut the door behind her and stooped to stroke his head, as people do when they are, perhaps, a little shy. Alistair set down his glass and hoisted himself to his feet.

'You remember Henrietta, don't you?'

He said, 'Yes, of course.' But he didn't. This was somebody totally new. Tall and slender, her hair wrapped close to the delicate shape of her head, one or two tendrils escaping to frame her features. She wore a long dress with a tall collar that emphasised her elegant neck. Her eyes were deep-set and dark; her mouth smudged with dimples when she smiled.

'Hello, Alistair.' She came toward him and gave him a kiss on his cheek. 'I'm sorry I'm late. I was working and I lost track of time. And then I was so grubby I had to go and have a bath. How lovely to see you again.'

He said, 'You've grown up.'

'Of course I have.'

'It's just that all the rest of the family are so exactly the same, I thought you would be too.'

'I'm sorry to disappoint you.'

'I'm not disappointed,' he told her.

They dined in what used to be the gloomy morning room, which Mrs Randall had turned into a countrified kitchen. There was a pine dresser, loaded with patterned china, baskets hanging from the ceiling, and a long scrubbed table. They ate homemade soup, and then pheasant with all the delicious trimmings, and a gooseberry fool. When this was finished, Mrs Randall made coffee, and Dr Randall went off to investigate the recesses of some cupboard and returned with a bottle of Drambuie.

'I haven't had such a meal,' said Alistair, 'since . . .' he tried to think, and ended up, 'since I went away, all those years ago.'

'You must come back,' said Mrs Randall. Over dinner, he had told them about his firm's plans. 'I really think it's time you wiped the dust of London from your feet and came back to us all.'

But he knew he could not commit himself. He looked around the table at the smiling faces turned toward him, the candlelight, the steaming cups of coffee, the golden glint of the liqueur and told himself that this was simply an interlude. One delightful evening with old friends could never be reason enough to dig up one's roots, to leave forever a person like Maggie.

When he'd been in his early twenties with everything in front of him, this had been enough. But he had been away for a long time. It wasn't always a good thing to turn back. However much one wanted it, things could never be quite the same.

He looked up, and realised that for once they were all quiet, watching him. He pulled himself together. 'Yes, perhaps. But I have a life in the south too. Commitments.' His glance moved, and all at once he met Henrietta's eyes. She was turned from the sink, her rubber-gloved hands slowly scrubbing a saucepan. A revelation struck him: *She's beautiful.*

'You talk as though you were a middle-aged man with a home and a family,' said Mrs Randall. 'It's not even as though you're married.'

Henrietta turned back to the sink, and set the saucepan on the draining board. The back of her neck seemed to Alistair as vulnerable as a child's. He said, 'No, I'm not even married.'

———◦———

When Alistair said that it was time to go, the old kitchen clock pointed only to eleven o'clock. But he had a long drive ahead of him the next day, and he knew that the Randalls' workday started earlier than most.

Janey's husband offered to run him back to the hotel, but Alistair refused his kind offer and said that he would walk. 'I've had no fresh air all day.'

In the hall he found his coat and said goodbye to them all. He kissed Mrs Randall and Janey, shook hands with the men.

He looked for Henrietta, and saw her emerging from a door at the end of the hall, buttoning up an old tweed overcoat, and carrying a lead for the dog.

'I'll walk with you a bit of the way,' she said. 'Charles has to go out anyway.'

So they went together, out into the still, cold night. They fell into step, Henrietta's long legs matching Alistair's pace, pausing every now and then while Charles sniffed at suspicious lampposts.

After London, it seemed amazingly quiet. Their footsteps rang on the icy pavement as they walked.

She said, 'It must seem very different from London. And funny to come back.'

'Not so much funny as disconcerting. Any place where you spent a fair amount of your youth is bound to be disconcerting.'

'Why is that?'

'Dreams, I suppose. Plans. You suddenly remember them all over again.'

'What were your dreams?'

'Making a million. Driving a Porsche. The usual.'

'Did they come true?'

'No.'

'Does that matter?'

'Not in the least. The great thing is that the important things haven't changed.'

After a little pause Henrietta said, sounding as if she were making a confession, 'That's what I'm afraid of. Things changing. Sometimes I feel so feeble. I mean, I've always lived here. I was born here, and I went to school here, and now I'm at art college here and I don't ever want to go away. All the girls I was at school with rushed off to London or America or Paris, and they think I'm the most ineffectual sort of person because I don't really want to go anywhere.' She looked at Alistair and smiled anxiously. 'Perhaps there's something wrong with me.'

'I don't see why. If you're happy in a place, why can't you just stay there?'

'I thought when I've finished this course, I might go to Australia. A girlfriend of mine is going.'

'What'll you do when you get there?'

'I could work in a shop or something.'

'I must say, you don't sound enthusiastic.'

'It's just that I don't really want to go.'

A thought struck him. 'Suppose,' he said slowly, 'suppose you met some chap and he wanted to marry you, and you wanted to marry him, and he was going to spend the rest of his life in Timbuktu. He was going to sell real estate in Timbuktu. What would happen then?'

Henrietta considered this problem as they walked in silence. 'I haven't even thought about marrying,' she told him at last. 'I can't imagine loving a man so much that I'd want to spend the rest of my life with him.'

'Imagine it now.'

'And he's going to sell real estate in Timbuktu?'

'That's the position.'

'Well, of course, I'd go.'

'The Timbuktu bit wouldn't put you off?'

'Well, yes, it would dreadfully. But if I wanted to spend the rest of my life with this man, then I wouldn't be happy anywhere else. So I might as well go.'

'You wouldn't be lonely?'

'If you've got a friend, you're never lonely. And a husband's meant to be a friend. At least, that's what I've always thought.

That's the way my parents are. Janey and George too. They never stop talking and giggling away together. That's the way I'd like to be.'

They had come to the main road, the traffic lights. Charles suddenly decided that he had walked far enough, and sat firmly on his haunches, so Henrietta stopped too. She said, 'This is as far as we usually come. That's why he's sitting down.'

'Then you must go back. You'll be all right?'

'Yes, of course. It . . . it seems a little unfriendly to say goodbye right here.' Lamplight shone on her face. A gust of wind wrapped a long tendril of hair against her cheek.

'Not unfriendly at all.'

She hesitated, then, sounding as shy as the child he remembered, said, 'It was great seeing you again. We all loved it.' She stood on tiptoe and kissed his cheek, then turned down the hill, walking, then running, with the dog galloping at her heels to keep up with her.

He watched until she was swallowed into the darkness. He crossed the street and went on, over the brow of the hill. He stood and looked up at the castle, crouched in the darkness like a sleeping lion. There were lights spangled all the way up the hill of the Old Town, and the trees' bare branches shivered in the bitter wind.

How old was Henrietta? Twenty. But she had known, instinctively, what he and Maggie, for all their sophistication, had been too blind to see. That if it was right between two people, it didn't matter where you lived. If Maggie didn't want to come to Edinburgh with him, then she didn't love him enough to want to spend the rest of her life with him. And he, terrified of making a mistake, had clung to his relationship with her as though it had been some sort of emotional lifeboat. But the truth was that it was simply a relationship. Amusing, rewarding, delightful, but nothing more.

Darling, I'm late, I'm late . . .

It was too cold to stand still. He turned and started toward the hotel. He walked with a purpose, a man who knew where he was going. Tomorrow he would return to London. It would take some weeks to tie up the details of the new office. He would have to find premises, choose a staff, look for a place to live. He would have to say goodbye to his friends. He would, finally, have to say goodbye to Maggie.

He was visited with a mental image of her, struggling into the Candide with her bundles, apologising, looking fantastic. And he smiled, because the very thought of her had always filled him with affection. But it wasn't enough, and already it seemed as though she belonged to another life.

He was coming back to live and work in this cold, beautiful northern city. He did not quite know when or how his decision had been made. He only knew that the dividing of the ways was behind him. So much lay ahead that he didn't think too much about Henrietta. Sooner or later, though, they would come together again. He hoped that she would wait for him, because he had a feeling that this time it would probably be for good.

The Stone Boy
(The Winds of Chance)

Arriving at night – met at the airport by her cousins, Julie and Harry, and driven the ten kilometres or so to the villa – there was no way for Liz to gauge the countryside or assess her new surroundings. She'd never been to this particular Mediterranean island before, and all was unfamiliar, yet not entirely strange. The velvet-blue darkness she remembered from other holidays, as well as the constant chirp of cicadas, and the smell of pine and juniper.

Even the villa was something of a mystery. Harry parked the car some distance from the dark shape of the house. A string of lights illuminated a path that descended in a series of small flights of steps. Julie led the way, and Liz followed, carrying her flight bag. Harry brought up the rear, with her suitcase and the raincoat she had needed in London.

In front of the house ran a terrace crowded with terracotta pots filled with flowers. Julie switched on a light, and all at once everything was floodlit like a stage set, but this brilliance only intensified the surrounding darkness, and it was impossible to imagine what lay beyond.

From the terrace, a door led into the house. This was not a modern villa, but a rustic island dwelling that Julie and Harry had recently bought and renovated. The night was warm, but the thick-walled interior, with red-tiled floors and white walls, felt cool.

There were huge sofas and chairs upholstered in white

canvas, bright cushions and rugs. At one end of the room, a fireplace contained the ashes of some bygone fire; at the other end stood a long scrubbed-pine table, surrounded by simple wooden rush-seated chairs.

Julie said, 'Now . . . would you like something to eat?'

'It's nearly midnight.'

'No matter. I can rustle up some food if you're hungry.'

'I'm not hungry. Just tired.'

'Bed, then.'

Julie led the way up a narrow staircase, the riser of each step faced with tiles. There were flowers everywhere, and the floors were a natural wood, sometimes a little uneven. 'You're sleeping here . . .'

Liz followed Julie into a small room of charming simplicity. Dark beams barred the whitewashed ceiling; shutters closed over a small window. There were a few hooks for clothes, and an old carved chest with a mirror hung above it. Freesia stood in a glass mug, and a white cotton cover topped the narrow bed.

'It's not very smart, I'm afraid,' Julie went on, 'but it's not meant to be a smart house. The bathroom's down the hall, and there's a mosquito net over the bed. I'd advise you to use it. Now, you'll be all right?' She didn't wait for an answer, but gave Liz a kiss, and then said, 'We'll talk tomorrow.'

Left alone, Liz kicked off her shoes and felt the coolness of the tile beneath her feet. She went to the little window, folded back the shutters, and took deep breaths of the dark, scented air. Instantly, a mosquito introduced itself, whining around the room like a miniature jet. She went to the bed, turned back the cover, and unknotted the net, which dropped, in folds, to the floor. Not only had she never been to this island, but she'd never slept beneath a mosquito net before. She smiled, relishing the new experience.

———

It was ten o'clock before Liz woke and found the sun already high in the sky. She went to the window. In the bright, hot light of morning, all was revealed – and it was far better than she'd dared to expect.

Below, the terrace; to one side a small swimming pool, glittering turquoise in the brilliant sunshine. Steps led down to a garden that was surrounded by thick stone walls and shaded here and there with gnarled olive trees. Beyond this, an almond orchard sloped to a narrow country road. And across the road stood another small house, and then the sea. The air smelled of lemons. Filled with anticipation, Liz quickly turned from the window, put on a bathing suit, brushed her long dark hair, wrapped herself in a terry robe, slipped sunglasses into the pocket, and went downstairs.

There was no sign of Harry, but she found Julie in the little kitchen.

'Good morning.'

Julie turned from the sink. 'There you are! How did you sleep?'

'Like a log. I think mosquito nets are romantic.'

'Like a cup of coffee?'

'Adore one.'

'Me too. Let's take it down to the pool.'

Breakfast was a juicy orange and a cup of black coffee consumed in a shaded pavilion that served as a changing room for the pool. There were a number of brightly coloured chairs set around, and pots of scarlet geraniums, and at one end of the pool stood a charming stone statue of a boy, his head turned, playing a pipe.

'Where did you get that statue?' Liz asked, resettling into a chaise in the sun.

'I found it in an antique shop in the village. I think he's meant to be a sort of Cupid. When I saw him, I knew he was exactly what I needed out here.'

'It's a heavenly house. Do you own the orchard too?'

'Yes, and the other house across the road. We rent it out.'

'Is anyone there now?'

'Yes. A rather nice young man. He arrived a couple of days ago. All on his own. I went down to introduce myself and made sure he had everything he wanted, and he seemed very content. In fact . . .' Julie's voice became deliberately casual. 'We've asked our friends, the Hathaways, to dinner tonight. I want you to meet them. And I asked our lodger as well. I thought it might be more amusing for you.'

Liz raised her eyebrows. 'You aren't matchmaking again?'

'Of course not,' Julie said, but her cheeks were rosy, and Liz knew that her cousin had already started to scheme.

Julie was fifteen years older than Liz, in some ways more like an aunt than a cousin, and she took a proprietary interest in Liz's love life. She was constantly producing suitable men, and constantly disappointed by Liz's lack of interest in them. She seemed even more disappointed by Liz's determined focus on her work. Julie herself was maternal and domestic, and so happy in her marriage that she found it hard to understand how Liz's career could mean so much, despite the fact that she'd made such a success of it.

Starting as a typist, Liz had slowly climbed the ladder at a glossy fashion magazine until she was now, at twenty-nine, the editor of the beauty section. As her responsibilities had grown, so had her salary, and she'd made her way from a rented room to a basement flat, and finally to her own small house. She had a car. She had her independence. She needed nothing more.

Nothing more. Sometimes, when she was tired or depressed or another birthday loomed, she'd tell herself this, firmly, aloud: 'I have it all. I need nothing more.'

'It's just . . .' Julie persisted, 'That I don't like to think of you *never* marrying. It would be so lonely.'

'I like being alone. I'm with people all day.'

'But being with someone you love isn't being with people. It's like being with the other half of yourself.'

'Not everyone's as lucky as you.' Liz tried diverting the conversation. 'Where *is* Harry, by the way?'

'He's gone to the village on an errand. He'll be back for lunch. And anyway . . .' – Julie was not to be diverted – 'you have to think about your old age.'

'I'm not thirty yet. I don't want to think about my old age.'

'But you're gorgeous . . . yes, you are. You always have been. I can't believe that you've never been in love.'

'What a romantic you are.'

'Not even *once*?'

Liz lay back in her chair; she observed through her dark glasses, the length of the rippling pool. The stone boy stood at its end, silhouetted against the sky. She said at last, 'Yes. Once. But it's over.'

'Oh, Liz. Why?'

'I suppose because I wasn't prepared for the commitment . . . and if you give your heart to a man, you have to trust him not to break it.'

'Didn't you trust him?'

'I don't know. Perhaps I didn't trust myself. I couldn't bear to be so jealous and suspicious.'

'Why should you?'

'Because of his job. He was a photographer – always off on glamorous locations with a harem of gorgeous models. I know how that goes, Julie. I've been in the business for years. Far from home, off on shoots, people live by their own rules.'

'Were you going to get married?'

'We talked about it, but we never became officially engaged.'

'Was he in love with you?'

'Oh, Julie, I don't know. I suppose so.'

'And you?'

In love. She remembered the excitement of those days – the sudden ecstasy of a phone call, the feeling that she wanted to run everywhere, laughing over nothing across candlelit tables, walking together on sunlit pavements, smelling lilac on a city street, driving in his car with the sunroof open to the sky and the sensation that there was nobody in the world but the two of them.

Julie was waiting for an answer.

Liz smiled, ruefully. 'Again . . . I suppose so.'

'Oh, darling, I can't bear it. Did you finish it, or did he?'

'I did. He went away on location for three weeks, and I was torn to pieces, not just missing him, but imagining every sort of intrigue. I knew one of the models who'd gone with him, and by the time they came back, I could have strangled her long, slender neck with my bare hands. And they probably hadn't even looked at each other. I hated myself for feeling that way, and I knew I couldn't live with that sort of distrust.'

'Would it have been worse than losing him?'

'It would have been worse for him.'

'When did this happen?'

'A couple of years ago.'

'Do you still see him?'

'No. When it ended, he went off to work in America. He wrote to me, but I didn't reply.'

'Oh, Liz.'

'Don't sound so tragic. It's just one of those things that didn't work. He's probably happily married by now. Don't let's talk about him any more.' She pulled off her dark glasses and sat up. 'I'm too hot to lie here another moment. Let's swim.'

That evening, Liz was at her mirror, coiling her hair into a chignon, when she heard the Hathaways arrive. From the terrace below, voices floated up; then came the sound of chairs being drawn forward, the clink of glasses. She fastened the tiny button at the neck of her caftan, sprayed some scent, fixed her earrings, then turned from the mirror and went, sandal-footed, down the stairs.

Outside, the terrace was an island of bright light surrounded by fragrant darkness. When Liz appeared in the doorway, the men got to their feet and Julie introduced her.

'This is my cousin, Liz. Meet Ken Hathaway – he's a sculptor – and his wife, Helen. Come sit down, darling.'

'You're looking marvellous,' said Helen Hathaway. 'Not burned at all. Just tanned. Usually visitors take too much sun the first day.'

'I'm careful.' Liz smiled and turned to take a tall iced drink from Harry.

'Now we're waiting for our final guest,' Julie said. 'He's our lodger, Helen.'

'*Really?*' Helen said, arching her brows.

'Don't say *really* like that. He's quite personable.'

'All on his own?'

'Yes, a very self-contained sort of person. Interesting, I thought. I hope he doesn't forget to come.'

'He hasn't forgotten,' Liz said, glimpsing the pale blur of a man's white shirt approaching by way of the orchard and the pool. As he passed the stone boy and moved into the light from the terrace, his figure – slight, fair-haired – took shape.

He climbed the steps to the terrace and, now stood in full light.

Julie sprang to her feet. 'Oh, how nice to have you with us. You know my husband, Harry . . . and this is Ken and Helen Hathaway. Meet John Lippiatt. And my cousin Liz Searley, who's staying with us.'

He shook hands all around, coming at last to Liz.

'How do you do,' she said quietly, and his hand closed around hers. This surprised her, because she had no recollection of putting it out to greet him.

He said, 'Liz Searley. How nice to meet you.'

'And now, John,' said Harry, 'what would you like to drink?'

———

They ate indoors, sitting around the long, candlelit table. For the occasion, Julie had cooked her famous paella, and there was homemade bread and huge wooden bowls of salad.

All through dinner, conversation bubbled, oiled perhaps by the copious amounts of local wine they were drinking, but Liz said little, content to listen.

Afterward, drinking coffee on the terrace, she found herself sitting next to the fair-haired young man. At dinner he'd told them little beyond his immediate circumstances . . . he'd needed a holiday, liked being alone. Ken had accused him of having a wife and brood of children whom he'd abandoned, but John had assured them that this wasn't the case.

'How long are you here for?' Liz asked him now, stirring her coffee, not looking into his face.

'Only a week. I can't take more time.'

'You must be a busy man. Where are you working?'

'In Paris just now.'

'Paris? That sounds exciting.'

'Yes, it is.'

'And what do you do all day?'

'Swim. Sit around. Paint.'

'*Paint?*'

He smiled. 'Yes, I started about a year ago. It's wonderful therapy.'

'I see.'

'What do you do with yourself in this marvellous place?' he asked.

'I've only been here a day.'

'The sun suits you. You should live in the sun.'

For some reason, Liz could think of nothing to say to this.

———◦———

At the end of the evening, the Hathaways said lengthy good-byes, then made their way home, escorted by Harry. Then John Lippiatt set down his empty coffee cup and said that he, too, must take himself off. He kissed Julie, formally, on the cheek, then turned to Liz. 'Good night,' he said. He did not kiss her. Smiling, he left the way he'd come, disappearing into the darkness beyond the stone boy.

Julie turned and began to stack the coffee cups. 'A nice man.'

'Yes,' Liz answered neutrally. 'And a heavenly evening. Thank you so much.'

Julie straightened, and her eyes met Liz's. 'I said, a nice man.'

'Of course. Delightful. Now, if you don't want me to do anything, I'm going to bed.'

'Good night, darling.'

'Good night. And thank you again.'

———•◦•———

Cocks crowing and the clamour of goat bells awakened her early. Liz reached for her watch and saw that it was only a quarter past seven. *I should go back to sleep*, she told herself, but was instantly wide awake, knowing that she must be up and about, out of doors in the pearly cool of the new day.

Five minutes later, she was standing beside the pool, undoing the sash of her robe. She poised and dived, shattering the surface of the water like broken glass. She swam a length and then another, back to the shallow end. She was standing, smoothing back her wet hair with her hands, when a voice said, 'Good morning.'

He seemed to have appeared out of nowhere, to stand by the stone boy and observe her. He wore a pair of swimming trunks, and his feet were thrust into shabby leather sandals.

'You're up early,' she told him.

'So are you.'

'The cocks crowing woke me.'

'They make a din, don't they?' He kicked off his sandals, and dove in, swimming toward her. When he stood beside her, she saw the strength of his body, the hard muscles beneath his tan, the blueness of his eyes spiked with wet, black lashes.

'Are the others up yet?' he asked.

'I don't think so.'

'Come with me, and I'll give you breakfast. Fresh melon and boiled eggs. The sun's on my terrace, and everything's smothered in bougainvillea.' When she hesitated, he went on, coaxing.

'Coffee, as much as you can drink. Fresh bread and orange-blossom honey. You can swim in the sea – that'll make a nice change. Sunbathe on a bed of bougainvillea. No woman could want more.'

'You don't need to get carried away. You're only asking me to breakfast.'

'Then you'll come?'

She swam away from him. 'Yes, I'll come,' she told him over her shoulder.

She followed him down the narrow path that wound beneath the almond trees, then across the road and through a gate into the tiny garden of the little house. The bougainvillea was indeed a sight, covering the terrace and clambering up on to the red tile roof.

'Come inside.'

The door was open, but hung with a brightly coloured curtain of beads that he held aside for her. Sunlight filled the place, and she saw that the house was, in fact, only a single room, with kitchen equipment at one end, and a bed, a table and two chairs.

He said, 'I'll make coffee,' and went to fill the kettle. He took down cups and saucers, and a jar of coffee, all his movements neat and economical. The simple room was starkly shipshape, and she saw that he had already made his bed. Next to it was a small table with a lamp and a pile of paperbacks, and a photograph in a leather frame. A photograph of a young woman with long dark hair, laughing, her eyes full of amusement and affection. *A photograph of herself.*

<hr />

She felt, quite suddenly, shaken and shocked. She knew that he wasn't married because he'd told them so last night, but she'd never expected that he would still keep her picture by his bed. Trembling, she went across the room, meaning perhaps to take the photograph from the table, to use it in some way as a weapon against him, but her legs suddenly felt wobbly and she sat down on the edge of the bed.

Surely there was something to say, some crisp and amusing observation that would snap the tension of the moment and put everything into perspective. Perhaps there was, but she couldn't think of it, and it was he who finally broke the silence.

He said, 'It goes everywhere with me. It has ever since you refused to see me again. I wanted you to know.'

'I thought it was my charming company you were after.'

'That too.'

'I thought you'd be married by now.'

'I thought the same about you. Did you never find what you were after?'

'I think I stopped looking.' She looked up at him. 'How long did you stay in America?'

'About eighteen months. Then I got a contract with a French magazine.'

'You're happy?' she asked. 'I wanted you to be happy.'

'Pity you weren't prepared to take the responsibility yourself.'

'That's not fair.'

'Why didn't you answer my letter?'

'I nearly did. I started to write, but I couldn't think of the right words, so I tore it up and threw it away. It wasn't any good, John. I wanted all of you for myself, and hated myself for feeling that way. Possessiveness smothers. I didn't want to smother you.'

'The truth is, you didn't trust me.'

'No.' She looked down, ashamed. It was a horrible thing to have to say.

He abandoned the kettle and crossed the room to sit beside her on the bed. 'What didn't you trust? Did you think every time I left you I'd start a new relationship? Or did you think I might not come back?'

'I suppose I . . .' She felt as though she were digging for the truth. 'I couldn't imagine any woman not wanting you the way I did.'

He took this calmly. 'Luckily we don't inspire the same reactions in every new person we meet. Otherwise the world would be in a sorry mess.' He smiled. 'Oh, Liz,' he told her, 'we'd have made a great team.'

'I would have made you miserable.'

'I'd rather be miserable with you than without you.'

Ridiculously, her eyes filled with tears. She half expected him to touch her, embrace her, even if only for comfort. And she realised then that this was what she wanted, more than anything in the world. Two years ago, she had turned her back on him, but he was still the most attractive, most compelling man she'd ever known. Nothing had changed, except, somehow, she was no longer so afraid.

He said, 'Did you tell your cousin about us?'

Liz shook her head.

He went on. 'When I saw you last night, sitting there on the terrace with the light on your hair, I thought for a moment that I was dreaming. Coincidence is an extraordinary thing. Why do you think we met again? Was it just by chance or was it planned by some higher authority? Did the gods decide they'd had enough, and it was high time we had our thick heads knocked together?'

'You never had a thick head. Mine was the thick one. I was quite stupid.'

'But so beautiful.' He shook his head. 'I never stopped loving you.'

A whistling sound came from the direction of the stove. They both ignored it. She said, 'I know. I see that clearly now, I think I'd rather be miserable with you than without you too.'

'We won't be miserable. We'll be blissful. It would be foolish to pass up this second chance. What do you say, Liz? Shall we grab it with both hands?'

She considered this a moment, then faced him. 'No commitments, no promises?'

He nodded. 'An open-ended agreement.'

Solemnly, they shook hands. She said, 'Do you know something?'

'Yes.' He put a hand on either side of her head, drew her face toward his, and began to kiss her. 'The kettle's boiling.'

———•◦•———

The sun was high in the sky by the time they made their way back through the orchard to the big house. Here, it was shady, light filtering through the trees, but the pool basked in full sunlight. By the statue of the stone boy, they paused.

'Julie said she thought he was a sort of Cupid. A little god of love,' Liz said.

John gave the little figure a pat on its stone bottom. 'Whoever he is, he's brought us luck.'

Julie appeared on the terrace above them, wearing a huge straw hat and wielding a large red watering can. When she saw them, she paused in her labours. 'There you are!' she called down to them. 'What have you been up to?'

They left the stone boy and went up the steps to tell her.

A Touch of Magic

It was a lovely June afternoon and Clare Ridley, with Aunt Jessica in her wake, carried a tray of iced tea out on to the patio.

'Where are the children?' Aunt Jessica asked in her deep voice.

'Playing somewhere with their friends.'

'And Howard?'

'He had an appointment in town.'

'Poor man, downtown on a day like this.' She lowered herself gingerly into a deck chair. All Aunt Jessica's movements were deliberate and cautious, not only because she was approaching seventy, but because she was large. Not fat, exactly, but tall and stately. In her colourful, mismatched clothing, she reminded Clare of a beautiful Bohemian.

Jessica was not Clare's aunt, but Howard's, and she lived only a mile from the Ridleys' in a small enviable house with a large well-tended garden. She had lived there most of her life, alone, because she had never married.

'Now,' said Aunt Jessica, coming right to the point, 'what did you want to talk to me about?'

Clare handed her a glass of tea. 'Josh is coming for the weekend.'

Aunt Jessica glanced up. 'Oh.'

'That was exactly my reaction.'

The two women sat in brooding, sympathetic silence. Josh

was Howard's brother and, if not exactly a black sheep, had all his life posed certain problems.

The inherited artistic streak, which ran like a fine thread through generations of their family, had come out in both brothers. In Howard it had taken a practical form, meanwhile Josh was a true artist – a painter – with all the charm, temperament, and instability that that single word can conjure up.

'Josh needs a wife,' Aunt Jessica said flatly.

It was an opinion shared by Clare, but now, after years of trying to interest Josh in settling down, she had made up her mind that it was hopeless. 'Time's run out, Aunt Jessica.'

'He wouldn't look at her,' Clare said. 'He has only to look at the right sort of girl and he runs like the wind.'

'I've been thinking about that,' Aunt Jessica said, her eyes sparkling with mischief. 'It's because he's an artist, with an artist's perception. Now if his visual attention could be caught—' She paused, a small smile lighting up her face. 'You must all come to lunch on Sunday.'

'Aunt Jessica, are you plotting?'

'Of course not, dear,' she said, with a hurt expression. 'I just want to have all my family together on Sunday.'

———◆———

From the end of the yard came the sound of a gate opening and shutting. The next moment Clare's children appeared in jeans and T-shirts and faded sneakers, looking dirty, red-faced and happy.

'Hello, Aunt Jessica,' said nine-year-old Katy and came to give her a kiss.

Danny, at eight years old, detested being kissed. 'Hello, Aunt Jessica,' he said, keeping a safe distance.

'What have you been doing to yourself?' Aunt Jessica asked him, noting the healing cuts on his knees and elbow.

'I was riding Charlie Taylor's bicycle and I fell off.'

'Why weren't you riding your own bicycle?' asked Aunt Jessica.

'It's so small.' All at once, and mostly for his mother's sake, his voice rose plaintively. 'I've been saving and saving for a new one, but I still need twelve dollars. I've just had a birthday so I've got to wait a whole year for some more money.'

'There's Christmas,' his mother reminded him.

'Christmas is ages away.'

Aunt Jessica tactfully changed the subject. 'You're all coming over for lunch on Sunday.'

'Oh, good. Can we go on the lake?' Katy asked.

Aunt Jessica's garden had a small lake in the middle of it, once created for some wealthy gentleman to stock with trout. But for the children it was the best treat in the world to be allowed into the old boat to row themselves around in circles pretending to be explorers.

'If it's a fine day,' Aunt Jessica promised.

<hr />

By Friday morning Clare was ready for Josh's arrival, and by Saturday morning she was fuming. How like him not to call to warn them he would be late. When the doorbell finally rang late in the afternoon, Clare jerked open the door, anxious to unleash her anger, but one look at Josh standing there, looking familiar and dear, and the words died in her throat.

'Clare,' he said, reaching out to hug her. 'You look marvellous.'

'So do you,' she told him and it was almost true. He was tan and healthy, but he was older. He needed a haircut and she saw the first hint of grey at his temples. There were smudges beneath his pale blue eyes. In faded jeans, a frayed plaid shirt, and sagging corduroy jacket, he looked more like a penniless waif than an internationally known painter.

From the rest of the family, he received a rapturous welcome. They were all so fond of him, Clare thought, as the children flung themselves into his arms and Howard's face lighted with joy at seeing his brother again.

Everyone helped to carry the luggage to the guest room and to assist in opening the suitcases. Out came photographs, ill-matched socks, books, magazines, and un-washed shirts. In no time the room had been taken over by his possessions and his towering personality. Clare gathered up a bundle of laundry and went to put it in the washer before serving drinks on the patio.

Minutes later Josh leaned back in his chair and stretched, turning his face up to the warm setting sun. 'Why do I ever go away?' he said.

A moment's hesitation, and then Clare said, 'Why do you?'

'I don't know.' He sounded hopeless. 'For the life of me. I don't know.'

———

But after dinner, with a cup of coffee in front of him, Josh opened up to Howard and Clare. He was getting too old, he told them. Too old to keep up with the pace of a life which he had set up as a student. Now, the physical labour of painting, the loneliness of his work, drained him of energy; and yet, because it was expected of him, he found himself partying half the night – expected to go here, there, and everywhere.

'Then stop it,' Howard told him bluntly. 'Learn to say "no".'

'It's more complicated than that. When I think about changing even one facet of my lifestyle. I have the classic painter's nightmare: the genius will disappear, my fingers will get stiff, my eye will falter.'

'But you don't need to change yourself,' Clare told him. 'If you just had a home of your own, then you wouldn't be at the mercy of all those creative, eccentric people you are expected to work with.'

'You mean a little woman?'

'You make it sound so banal.'

'If I could find a little woman like you, it would be easy.'

'You wouldn't last a day with a woman like me.'

'I suppose I wouldn't.' He sounded sad. And then he yawned, looking at his watch, and announced he was going to bed.

It rained in the night, and the next morning the world was

hazy with mist. But as the sun rose, it burned the mist away, and by the time they left for Aunt Jessica's it was a hot and breezy day.

In ten minutes they were there, turning in through the open gate and driving up the short curve of the drive that bordered the little lake. There were deck chairs set out on the lawn, and Aunt Jessica was waiting for them. Clare saw, with a start of surprise, that there was someone with Aunt Jessica. A young woman in a brown skirt and beige blouse. Her hair had been bundled casually into a soft knot at the back of her head. The effect was distinguished, but colourless. Clare wondered what Aunt Jessica was up to. Did she think this was a woman to capture Josh's visual attention?

'Josh!' Aunt Jessica came forward to embrace him. 'I'm so happy to see you.'

She stepped back and circled her arm around the young woman's shoulders, propelling her forward. Before she could speak, the woman said shyly, 'Hello, Josh.'

'Good lord!' he said. 'Elizabeth Kennedy.'

'I didn't think you'd remember me.'

'Of course I remember you. How are you?' He grasped her hand warmly. 'What are you doing here?'

'My father retired here. He hasn't been well lately and I've come to live with him. I've been writing children's stories since I graduated from school. It's work I can do anywhere.' She turned to greet Howard and Clare. 'Josh and I met in college,' she explained. Her smile transformed her face. *Why, she's beautiful*, Clare thought.

They settled into chairs to drink wine outdoors, but went inside to eat lunch. Crowded around the polished oak table, they feasted on chicken and roast potatoes. The conversation never faltered, but Clare was silent. Across the table Elizabeth and Josh sat side by side. It occurred to Clare that if Josh really wanted to settle down, Elizabeth Kennedy would be perfect for him. She was intelligent and self-contained. They had memories to share and they would share the same sort of friends. More importantly, they would balance each other. Her calm aura of quiet efficiency would soothe his mercurial temperament, and his vitality would fire response into that pale, quiet, dark-eyed face. It needed something to bring it to life. A touch of makeup, a touch of sunlight, a touch, perhaps, of love?

Clare looked at the long clean line of Elizabeth's throat, the neat tilt of the small nose. *She is beautiful*, she thought again. *She really is beautiful.*

After lunch they returned outside. Howard was deep in a deck chair, reading the Sunday paper. Josh had taken himself off to a distant and sheltered corner and was fast asleep on the lawn.

'Unsociable devil,' muttered Aunt Jessica.

From across the smooth water of the lake came the creak of oars as Katy painfully rowed the old boat. Elizabeth was her passenger. Danny waited at the water's edge for his turn.

'Hurry up, Katy!'

Aunt Jessica walked down to the little boy. 'Don't be impatient,' she told him. 'You'll get your turn.' She pulled him down to sit beside her on the grass, under the shade of a frilly parasol that she always carried in sunny weather. Their voices sank to a companionable murmur.

The prow of the boat bumped against the pier and Danny rushed to take the oars. There was a great deal of splashing and shouted instructions, but finally he got himself settled, and Elizabeth was once more on her way around the lake.

It was all very peaceful. But suddenly, the drowsy afternoon was pierced by a shriek from Danny. 'Look!' he cried, jumping to his feet. The boat rocked violently, he lost his balance and, trying to save himself, trod heavily on the gunwale. The next moment, the boat tipped and turned. There was a splash and both Elizabeth and Danny disappeared into the water.

Clare and Howard sprinted for the water's edge. Elizabeth and Danny stood waist deep on the muddy, shallow bottom, gasping for breath. Elizabeth pushed long strands of wet hair from her face and started to laugh.

'You will both have to get out of those wet clothes,' Aunt Jessica said when everybody and everything had been hauled back on to dry land.

'I think I'd better go home,' said Elizabeth, wringing out the hem of her skirt.

'And you should go home too,' Howard told his son. 'I've never seen you do anything so idiotic.'

But Aunt Jessica would have none of it. 'Rubbish,' she said. 'There's no harm done. I can find something for Elizabeth to wear. Stop scowling, Howard, accidents happen.' She took Elizabeth's arm. 'Come along, dear . . .'

Clare found a pair of old swimming trunks in the car and handed them to Danny. 'I thought you know never to stand up in a boat. Why did you do such a silly thing?'

'I thought I saw a big fish.'

'Well, if you see another fish, don't stand up.'

'No,' he said, 'I won't.'

Katy and Howard were in the boat, baling out the last of the murky water. Josh had slept through it all.

Fifteen minutes later the back door opened, and Clare, turning to apologise to Elizabeth for her son's carelessness, was struck speechless. For with Aunt Jessica was a very different woman – tall and elegant in a long, flowing gown of ruffles and lace. It was one of Aunt Jessica's dramatic timeless relics of the past. The skirt flowed from Elizabeth's narrow waist and gently brushed her ankles. The splash of colours brought a glow to her cheeks. She looked sensational.

Clare found her voice at last. 'Elizabeth!'

'You look like a princess,' Katy said.

'Well, thank you,' said Elizabeth. She picked up Aunt Jessica's parasol and raised it above her head. 'I think this adds the finishing touch, don't you? And now who's going to take me out in the boat again?'

'You mean you want to go out again?' Danny asked.

'Of course. If I'm dressed up like this. I have to go out again. You and Katy can both be my gondoliers, but if you rock the boat, I promise to hit you with my parasol.'

'I won't rock,' Danny promised. 'I won't rock this time.'

They were all out in the middle of the lake before Josh woke. He yawned and sat up, rubbing a hand across his eyes, pushing back his hair from his forehead. He saw the scene before him: the water, the reeds, the distant trees and sky. And framed in all of this, the boat, and the girl in her lace dress with the parasol held high over her head.

'Good lord!' He got to his feet and went slowly down to the water's edge. He could only look at the girl in the boat, afraid that if he stopped staring she would disappear. He reached into his pocket to find the piece of charcoal, and the sketch paper he was never without. An almost visible impulse flowed from his eyes down to his fingers. He began to draw.

———

At the end of the day the family went home alone because Josh and Elizabeth had drifted off in the direction of Aunt Jessica's rose garden and did not reappear again.

'Leave them,' advised Aunt Jessica, her face aglow.

Clare could only smile and shake her head in wonder.

At eight o'clock that night the telephone rang. It was Josh. Josh, who never called to explain where he was or if he'd be late.

'Clare. I'm with Elizabeth. We're going out for dinner.'

'I'll leave the front door open for you.'

'Bless your heart.' His voice sounded young again and full of life.

Smiling thoughtfully, Clare replaced the phone and went upstairs to see her son. Danny was almost asleep. She moved cautiously across his littered room and sat on the edge of his bed.

He put out his hand and she took it in hers.

'I want to ask you something *very special*,' he told her.

She waited.

'Tomorrow after school, would you take me down to the bike shop?'

'But Danny . . . you don't have enough money yet.'

'Yes, I have.'

She stared at him. He reached under his pillow and pulled out a little fistful of riches. 'Aunt Jessica gave it to me. I did something for her and she paid me.'

'What did you do?' Clare asked, but she knew.

His face, against the pillow, was innocent.

'I upset the boat,' he said.

Despite herself, Clare began to laugh. 'Oh Danny. Bless *your* heart. And Aunt Jessica's too!'

A Smile for the Bride
(also published as '*Oh Heavenly Day*' in
Good Housekeeping)

Amelia awoke at six o'clock. It happened suddenly, as though some person had shaken her, or an alarm bell had rung. Sunlight lay across her bed. The open window revealed a summer sky already blue, traversed by racing clouds. A wind thumped and nudged at the house, rattling her bedroom door and sending cotton curtains billowing like badly set sails.

She got out of bed and went, in her nightdress, to inspect the day. The tide was out. The estuary lay empty, a sheet of sand and mud, spattered with tide-pools which reflected the blue of the early sky. A pair of gulls were perched on the summerhouse roof, screaming their hearts out, and below, in the garden, her mother's syringa bush was heavy with fat, fragrant white blossom.

It was the same as any other summer morning, and yet it was like no other morning. In all the eighteen years that Amelia had lived at this house, the view from her window had remained unchanged. But, after today, she knew that it would never appear precisely the same. After today home would no longer be this shabby, comfortable, loved old house, it would be a tiny two-roomed flat off the Fulham Road, with a view from the front window of nothing more exciting than the houses opposite, and only a flagged yard at the back to make do for a garden. Because today, at half past eleven, in the ancient village church where she had been christened, Amelia was going to be married, and she would not be Amelia Bentley ever again, but Mrs David Easton.

The morning air was sweet and cold and smelled of the sea. The only sounds were the gulls' scream and the buffet of the wind. Within the house no person stirred. Amelia leaned on the sill of the open window and waited for significant emotions to stir in her breast. Surely a bride on her wedding morning should feel some special way. Romantic or excited, or even vaguely apprehensive. Amelia felt nothing only an irresistible urge to be on her own on such a beautiful morning, and, perhaps for the last time in her life, totally free.

She turned away from the window, pulled off her nightdress, and got dressed in ancient jeans, a pair of turn sneakers, and a sweater which had once belonged to one of her brothers — the only clothes which had not been mended, washed, ironed and packed in her honeymoon suitcases. She went out of the room and, soft-footed, down the stairs. In the hall stood the telephone and on the pad beside this she scribbled a note for her mother to find.

Gone out. Don't worry, back in good time to wash my hair. Amelia.

She propped this against the telephone, and then gently turned the key in the front door and let herself out.

Despite the sunshine, the wind was keen. She made her way around to the old shed behind the garage and collected her bicycle. The wind was behind her and she free-wheeled down the lane, and then turned into the road which led through the still slumbering early-morning village. She passed the church, set back from the road, the grassy churchyard filled with lichened, leaning gravestones. Yesterday they had spent the day filling the church with flowers, white roses and lilies and huge white daisies. Alongside it, behind a screen of trees, stood the rectory. She imagined the Reverend Davies, with his homely wife alongside him, asleep in their double bed.

She came to the gates of the manor, which used to be a real manor but was now a rather grand hotel, and where the reception after the wedding was to be held in something called a Function Room. The wedding cake, delivered the day before, would already be in position on an immense silver platter provided by the baker. Amelia and David, man and wife, would cut the first slice with her grandfather's old Naval sword. Amelia's mother had dug it out of some old chest, and her father had cleaned it of rust and oiled it with salad oil. Amelia hoped it would be sharp enough to get through that layer of delicious hard icing.

She cycled on. Past Miss Curtice's house – the general store – the butcher's. The butcher's blinds were still down, and the butcher's cat sat on the pavement in the sun and attended to his ablutions.

And then, at the end of the village, the little pub. The Clipper, whitewashed and thatched, with a grassy patch before it where, in the summer evenings, old men sat with their mugs of beer and ruminated peacefully on all aspects of life. This was where David, bowing to convention, had been banished for the night before his wedding. The night before that, after driving down from London, he had stayed with the Bentleys, and they had had a big family dinner party. But tradition seemed to insist that his last night of freedom should be spent apart from his bride-to-be.

Mrs Rodgers, who kept the pub, didn't – as she put it – take residents in the normal course of events but had been only too delighted to bend her rule for the important occasion and David had been given the best front room.

Cycling past the quiet inn, Amelia thought of him, asleep with his precious head on one of Mrs Rodgers' finest embroidered pillow-cases, his dark hair tousled, his face peaceful in sleep. She sent him a silent message, her heart filled with tender love. She wished, above everything, that he could wake up as instinctively happy as she had been, but she knew that he couldn't. It was such a little thing that had happened, but it was enough to cloud his day.

At that moment, appropriately enough, a cloud passed over the sun. The road ran downhill, beneath a dark tunnel of oak trees and, despite herself, Amelia's own bright spirits were dimmed. It wasn't any good telling herself that it didn't matter because it mattered so much to David, and so it mattered to Amelia. Right up to yesterday night, she knew that he had been hoping that at the last moment there would be a message from his Uncle Douglas to say that he had changed his mind, that he was flying home from New York and would be at their wedding. But there had been no word.

Nothing had been said, but last night, when she kissed him goodbye, they both knew in their hearts that his uncle would not be there.

Quite often uncles and nephews aren't all that close, but in David's case it was different. He was an only child. His father had died when he was a small boy and his mother when he was twelve. Since then there had been only Uncle Douglas. It was he who had seen David through school, sent him off to Australia for a couple of years, and then arranged for him to be articled to a firm of chartered accountants in order to qualify, and, in the fullness of time, join the investment company of which Uncle Douglas was chairman.

But he was, and had been for the past six months, on a mammoth business trip abroad. From Hong Kong he had gone to Tokyo, and was now in New York, deeply involved in the setting up of some new trust company, and Amelia — because the romance had all been such a blissful, whirlwind affair — had never met him.

So delighted were they with each other, so pleased were Amelia's family, so perfect was everything, that Uncle Douglas's reaction to David's news had the effect of a douche of cold water. It came in the form of a long and typewritten letter which in itself was chilling. Amelia imagined him dictating it to some heartless secretary, sandwiched between an annual balance sheet and a takeover bid.

It was unenthusiastic and strictly to the point. David was far too young. Twenty-two was no age to take on all the responsibilities of marriage. As well, David was still learning his trade, was not yet qualified, was scarcely earning enough to keep himself, let alone a wife. When – in two years' time – he had taken and passed his final examinations, the situation would be different. Until then, David was strongly advised to hold his horses, think again, and behave like a rational human being.

———◆———

Amelia, depressed and discouraged by this, had rung her mother to pass on the gloomy news. 'How can he be so mean? If he's fond of David as he makes out, why doesn't he want him to be happy?'

Mrs Bentley, distressed for her daughter but determined to be fair, had tried to comfort her without taking sides. 'Well, darling, you *are* both a little young.'

'Heaps of people get married when they're young. And we know it's right. As for money, I can go on working. Between us we'll be able to manage. I know we will.'

'Yes, you know that, but David's uncle doesn't.'

'But David *told* him.'

'Perhaps he feels that being married will interfere with David's studies.'

'Well, I think not being married would be much worse. I mean, he'd always be ringing me up or wanting to be with me instead of doing his beastly accounts.'

Her mother had sighed. 'Well, it's up to you. You and David. Nobody can decide but yourselves.'

Amelia had thought this over. Later: 'If you want,' she had

told David, 'if you think we should . . . I'd wait two years. I mean, I'd never fall in love with anybody else. I couldn't bear there to be any sort of ill-feeling between you and Uncle Douglas. In a way, he's your father, and I want him to like me. Not to think I've spoiled everything for you.'

'I couldn't wait two years,' David had said. 'Even if I thought we should. I couldn't.' He kissed her. 'He'll come round. He's never been a man to bear a grudge. And once he's met you, he'll understand. Everything will be different.'

For a man so young he had great determination and a mind of his own. He had written back to his uncle, telling him that the wedding date was fixed for July. A month before this, Amelia gave in her notice, left London, and went home to help her mother with the many arrangements. A dress was chosen, a list of guests made out. Invitations were printed and Amelia helped her mother to write them out, including one for Uncle Douglas. With this Mrs Bentley sent a little letter in which she said that she and her husband were looking forward to meeting him.

The reply to this missive was polite, but very formal. Pressure of work was considerable, and he regretted very much that he would not be able to be present. A day or two later, David received from him a hefty cheque – enough, and more, to pay for their honeymoon. For some reason this, as far as Amelia was concerned, only made everything worse.

'I wish he hadn't,' she told David. 'It makes me feel guilty.'

'Do you want me to send it back?'

'No, you can't do that. That would be really ungracious. It's just that I'd rather he came to the wedding than gave us a cheque. And it's horrid for you having nobody of your own there.'

'I shall have you,' David told her. 'I'd rather have you than a thousand relatives.'

———•·•———

By now, the village was left behind. The trees thinned out, the road leaned and twisted up towards the moor. The sun, freed once more of cloud, shone down upon the farmland. There were stone-walled fields; pastures filled with grazing cows; farm buildings with lichened roofs.

Then there was only moorland and heather and the whining of the wind. Gorse splashed the hedgerows with yellow flame, and above the road, and now quite close, lay the little hill, with its crown of massive rock. It became too steep to cycle any longer, and Amelia had to get off her bicycle and push it for the last half-mile. She reached the granite stile set in the wall, parked her bicycle, crossed the stile and set off up the last long ascent, following the path between bramble and bracken.

The wind was against her, drumming in her ears and rich with the scent of moss and the saltiness of the ocean. The gargantuan carn towered above her, hiding the sun. The path circled this immense, and possibly man-made fortress – and ended at last at the very top of the hill. Amelia scrambled up the rocks, and finally was there. The top of the world, she used to call it when she was a child. The view, on all sides, spread to the sea. She saw the distant beaches and the coastline curving away to the north. She saw the inlet of the estuary, the village, the tower of the church just visible through the trees.

There was a sheltered hollow in the rocks, out of the wind and good for sitting on.

A voice said, 'Oh, I do beg your pardon,' and Amelia nearly jumped out of her skin. 'And now I've given you a fright, so I shall have to beg your pardon all over again.'

He had come from behind her, having climbed the rock just as she had climbed it, but he was wearing thick rubber-soled shoes which made no sound. He stood there, only a few feet away, and looked just as surprised and upset as Amelia felt.

'It's all right.' Her heart was hammering, but he was so obviously distressed that the least she could do was to put him out of his misery. 'I never heard you coming.'

'And I had no idea you were here. At seven in the morning one doesn't expect company in such an out-of-the-way spot.'

For a second, Amelia had been truly frightened, but only for a second. There was nothing to be frightened of. Just an elderly gentleman, countrified and shabby, in a threadbare knickerbocker suit, a tweed hat, and carrying a pair of binoc-ulars slung around his neck on a leather strap. In one hand he held a stout stick, and the band of his hat was decorated with a colourful fishing fly or two. All this she found totally re-assuring. He was probably on a walking holiday, taking brass rubbings in the old churches, or watching for birds. Beneath bushy eyebrows was a pair of very bright blue eyes, and these disappeared into slits when he smiled, which he did now.

'If you like, I'll go away and leave you alone.'

'No, don't do that. I don't mind. Besides, this is the only spot where you can look at the view and be out of the wind.'

'Well, if you're sure you don't mind.' He looked about him, chose a handy spur of rock and settled himself down, laying his stick carefully beside him. 'It's quite a walk.'

'Are you staying nearby?'

'Yes. At The Castle Hotel. Just for the weekend. It's the first time I've been in this part of the world. The porter told me this would be a good walk and a rewarding view.'

'It's one of my favourite places.'

'You sound as though you might be a native of these parts.'

'Yes, I am. I live in that village down there in the trees. I cycled up, but I had to leave my bike at the stile.'

'The gorse is particularly beautiful. It smells of almonds.'

'And in spring there are thousands of primroses. When we were children we used to come up here every Easter. And when we'd picked great bunches of primroses we used to have a picnic and light a bonfire. It was a sort of tradition.'

'Traditions are good things, provided you don't let them get the upper hand. Are you on your holidays now?'

'Well, not actually. I mean I'm not working at the moment, but I suppose you can't call it a holiday. I did have a job in London, but I've given it up for the time being.' It sounded too confusing for words, and Amelia decided to tell him. 'The thing is, I'm getting married.'

This abrupt announcement was met with silence. After a little she added, 'Today,' like somebody putting a full stop to the end of a sentence. As soon as she had said it, she wished that she hadn't. He would say something courtly and embarrassing.

But he only remarked gravely, 'You astonish me.'

'Why?'

'You look too young to be getting married.'

'I'm twenty. David's uncle says it's too young.'

'David, I take it, is the young man you're marrying.'

'Yes. He's twenty-two.'

'But does it really matter what his uncle thinks? Uncles aren't, after all, that important in the normal structure of affairs.'

'David's uncle is different.'

———•—•———

And suddenly, without thinking very much about it, Amelia began to talk. It was an enormous relief to bring it all out into the open. Like talking to some unknown but tremendously sympathetic stranger one had met on a train, and knew that one would never meet again.

It all came out: about meeting David and falling in love, and deciding they wanted to get married. She told him about Uncle Douglas's letter, and the letter he had written to her mother.

'He said he was too busy to come to the wedding. Right up to last night, I think David thought he'd relent and that he'd come, but he obviously isn't going to. It's so sad, really. I'm sure if we'd been able to talk things over with him, face

213

to face, he'd have given us his blessing. It won't be easy financially, but we realise that. And I'll get another job, and if we save up we might even be able to make a down payment on a little flat.'

She added gloomily, 'It's awful starting your normal married life feeling the way I do about David's only relative. I can't even think about him as a person. Just a robot, sitting behind a desk with a face like an adding machine, and an electronic calculator for a heart.'

'You're getting on dangerous ground here. Preconceived ideas of people can be extraordinarily wrong.'

'I don't mind for me, but I do mind for David.'

'If you ask me, this uncle sounds a very proud and stubborn man. But if he has any sense at all, he'll swallow his pride and get into an aeroplane and be in the church today to see his nephew married.'

'It's too late for that,' said Amelia sadly.

'Don't be too sure. And don't have any regret or second thoughts about what you and your young man have decided to do. If you don't know your own mind, you're never going to know anybody else's. And now –' he smiled – 'I must be on my way. I've a long walk ahead of me and I don't want to miss my breakfast.' He got to his feet. 'So I'll leave you. I'm sorry to have disturbed your solitude. I shall be thinking of you this morning, and I wish you and your young man a very happy life.'

'Thank you. Goodbye.'

He turned and left her. Amelia watched him make his way

over the crest of the rock, and then the steep incline sloped away and he dropped out of sight. He was gone, headed back across the moor, with five miles to cover before he could sit down to his breakfast. The very thought of sitting down to breakfast made Amelia realise that she was ravenously hungry. It was time to go home.

She got to her feet. The sun was now quite high in the sky, the ocean blue as ink and crested with white horses. She had a last lingering look, and then turned and started the long walk to where she had left her bicycle.

On the way down the hill, she searched for her new friend, but he had already disappeared, swallowed up into the undulations of the moor. It was as though he had never existed, as though she had created him out of her own imagination, simply because she needed a sympathetic person to talk to, someone to reassure her that they had made the right decision.

***

And now it was time to leave for the church. Her three brothers were already there, ushering guests into their pews. Her mother and the bridesmaids had departed in the first of the hired cars, her mother looking suitably festive and only a little tearful about the eyes.

'Oh, Mother, you mustn't cry. Your mascara will run.'

'Well, you are my only daughter. This is an emotional day.'

They kissed and hugged, cautiously, so as not to crush their dresses. When they had gone there was another five minutes to wait (time for a quick glass of sherry, said her father, so they had a private drink together, with nobody watching) and then it was time for them to leave.

With her father's hand beneath her elbow, Amelia emerged once more from the house, into the sunshine and the wind. And there, waiting for her, was Mr Potter's taxi, adorned with white ribbons. And Mr Potter – who, in bygone days used to drive Amelia to dancing class – standing with a grin on his face like a slice of melon. They got into the car, and then, because the house was only about a hundred yards from the church, almost immediately got out of it again, and there were all sorts of interested and friendly village faces lined up, smiling at her from the roadside and the tops of walls.

'Oh, what a lovely bride . . .'

The wind caught her veil and sent it billowing as they passed beneath the lych-gate and started up the path towards the church. High above, the tower bells clanged and pealed, sending their cheerful message out across the countryside. And there, at the church door, the vicar waited, windblown in his white starched surplice. And the bridesmaids were there, and . . .

One of Amelia's brothers suddenly burst from the interior of the church and through the door, and came down the path towards them. Amelia supposed that he intended to help her father control her wayward veil, but he wore the expression of a man with important news to impart.

'Amelia – gosh, you look pretty – I've got a message for you from David. And he said I was to tell you before you set foot in church, and I had to be tactful otherwise you'd faint.'

Amelia's father, not unnaturally, by now was looking a little anxious. 'Well, come on, boy, get on with it.'

'The message was "Uncle Douglas is here".'

'What do you mean, he's here?'

'He's here in the church. Seems he flew from New York after all. Told David he'd had second thoughts. First David knew of it was when he suddenly saw the old boy advancing down the aisle towards him. Happened five minutes ago. David let out a great bellow of welcome, and the organist lost his place in "Sheep May Safely Graze", and with one thing and another, there's been quite a to-do. But David wanted you to know, and I've told you, and you haven't fainted. So now we can get on with it.' He gave her a quick, brotherly kiss. 'And you look smashing. You really do!'

'If he has any sense at all, he'll swallow his pride and get into an aeroplane and be in the church today to see his nephew married!'

———◦◦◦———

'You're not going to cry?' asked her father, anxiously inspecting his daughter's lovely face.

Uncle Douglas was here. David would have somebody at the wedding who belonged to him.

'I don't know,' whispered Amelia. For the first time she felt nervous. All at once she was shaking with nerves.

217

'You mustn't cry.' He remembered what Amelia had told her mother. 'Your mascara will run.'

So she didn't cry. And now they were in the church, and everybody was singing. On their feet, led by the choir, their voices cheerful and robust, filling the tiny church with a triumphant explosion of sound.

> '*Oh Worship the King,*
> *All glorious above.*'

Her father took Amelia's hand, tucked her arm into his. They moved forward. She could feel the whisper of her long silk skirts on the worn flagstones of the aisle. At the far end, standing facing her and wearing a grin that matched Mr Potter's, David waited. All nervousness suddenly evaporated. She smiled back, and then looked for Uncle Douglas.

She found him. A solitary figure in the front pew, singing away with the best of them. And there was no mistaking that upright and comfortable-looking figure, despite the fact that now he was dressed in formal wedding clothes and wore no hat upon his white-haired, balding head.

Uncle Douglas.

I knew it was you, that nice sympathetic man I met up on the hill this morning. I thought that Uncle Douglas would be cold and inhuman, with an electronic calculator for a heart. And you obviously thought Amelia was a stupid little featherhead without a notion of what she was letting herself in for. And by a miracle — by some heaven-sent chance — we've found out that both of us were wrong.

The little procession, moving slowly, came alongside the front pews. Amelia hesitated, halted and turned her head to look at him. He stopped singing and met her gaze. She saw the blue eyes, set deep beneath the shaggy eyebrows, and at this moment there was undoubtedly a most irreverent twinkle in them. She half-expected him to send her a conspiratorial wink, but he didn't. He smiled. Amelia smiled back, and he turned once more to his hymn sheet and went on singing.

She couldn't stop smiling. She was still smiling when she reached David's side; when she stood beside him; when she took his hand and knew all was well in their world.

Magic Might Happen

There are times in one's life that one remembers being good, even if they only last for a month or two, or even a week, or a couple of days. That summer was a good time. Like getting into a placid harbour after a stormy voyage, or touching down at some sunlit airport after a turbulent flight.

The storms, turbulence, call them what you will, had taken various forms. My father, Chairman of Crayshaw Floorings, had gone through some anxious months, totally taken up with the business of trying to steer his company through the rough seas of modernisation, internal relations and the economic recession. I had struggled through my last year at school, working for sufficient A levels to get me a place at university. I wanted this so badly that I swotted into the early hours of the morning, panicked over the amount of revising I had to do and lost a stone and a half in weight. I am a born worrier.

And finally, perhaps because of all this, my mother became ill, and was whisked into hospital for an operation which the doctor termed minor, but which didn't seem minor to us. The worst thing that can befall a family is to have its mother in hospital. The entire world becomes disoriented, the home has lost its heartbeat, there is no answer when you call.

But by the summer it was all over, Crayshaw Floorings survived, and even began, gradually, to prosper again. My father stopped falling into a chair and dropping off to sleep when he came home, and instead emerged into the garden to do constructive things like slaying slugs or dead-heading roses. I achieved the A levels but, best of all, my mother came home from hospital. She still had to rest from time to time, but she was *there*. You could smell her scent when you came into the house. You could hear her soft voice talking in the kitchen to Rosa, our Spanish cook. There were scones for tea again, and the house was filled once more with flowers.

Now, it was drawing towards the end of August. There was nothing more to worry about and the sun shone day after day. My father suggested a holiday, but my mother had already promised to visit her sister Charlotte in Sutherland, in September, so we stayed at home, just the three of us, and lay in the garden, did a little desultory gardening, and ate all our meals on the terrace.

We live in a largish and rambling old house, and the fact that it is really too big, with a garden that has been allowed to go half wild, is more than compensated for by the little river which flows gently around its boundary, willow-fringed and speckled with shafts of sunlight. Mostly it is shallow, chuckling and bubbling down in a series of small water splashes and little pools. But at one special place there is a pool deep enough to swim in. There is a rock there in the middle, usually covered by water, but now, after the dry weather, its smooth rounded surface lay dry and exposed, patterned with leaf shadows so that it looked like leopard-skin.

On this particular day I had spent the whole afternoon

there, alternately lying in the sun with a book, and wading into the cool brown water when I could bear the heat no more. Finally, as the shadows lengthened across the burnt-brown lawn, I pulled an old sundress over my bikini, picked up my book and made my way back to the house.

My mind was full of cool thoughts, cool images. A shower, perhaps; a Chopin prelude on the record player; the cold salmon I knew we were going to eat for supper. As I came up the sloping lawn I heard the telephone ring indoors and my mother answer it. In the fear that it might be someone to speak to me, I hung about the garden. When the telephone rang briefly once, and I knew that the call was finished, I went on into the house.

After the brightness outside, the hall was dim. My mother materialised as though out of darkness.

'Oh darling, that call was for you. Roger Marsden. He says will you ring him back?'

I knew a moment of quiet satisfaction that I had had the wit to delay my entrance. 'What does he want?'

Her voice pleaded slightly. She longed for me to be a social success, leading a life of perpetual dates and outings. I loved her very much and it was hateful to disappoint her, but no amount of telling could persuade her that I simply wasn't that sort of person: that if I was lost in a book, it was because I loved the book, not because I hadn't been asked out: that if I sat for hours at the grand piano in the sitting-room, practising and knowing that I could never achieve perfection, it was because this fulfilled and absorbed me more than an evening with Roger or indeed anyone else. I don't really like Roger.

'I said I don't want to go.'

'Now, why not? Roger's so nice . . .'

'Just because his mother and you are bosom friends it doesn't follow that Roger and I have to be too. I'm sorry but I don't want to go. I want to eat cold salmon with you and Dad. Besides, there's a gorgeous concert on television . . .'

'Victoria, you're eighteen. It's unnatural to be so unsociable.'

'Then you have mothered an unnatural child,' I said lightly. 'Perhaps I'm a foundling. Are you sure you actually had me and didn't find me in a laundry basket at the door?'

'Of course I had you. It's just that . . .'

'I know, I'm a disappointment to you.' I kissed her. 'Just try not to be disappointed. And I'll ring Roger and tell him I can't make it.'

At that moment the phone rang again startling us both, and my mother, with an exasperated glance in my direction, picked up the receiver and found it was my father ringing from the office. I sat on the stairs and listened, and because he always talks on the telephone as though they had never been invented, their two voices were entirely audible. In fact, my father's was more audible than my mother's.

'Diana.'

'Yes, darling?'

'Would it be all right if I brought a man home for dinner this evening and to stay the night?'

'But of course,' said my mother instantly, without taking

time mentally to measure up the cold salmon, or to start fussing about clean sheets. This is one of the things that I love about her. 'Who is he?'

'He's down from London. From Fleming Bernsteins, actually.'

My mother raised her eyebrows. 'That sounds exciting.'

'It might be. Don't start chattering about it, though.'

'When will you be home?'

'About seven. See you then.'

'Stephen!' called my mother in a panic, before he could ring off. 'What's he called, the man who's coming tonight?'

'John Stebbings,' said my father, and this time he did ring off.

My mother put down the receiver and looked at me, making a knowing face.

'At a guess,' I said, 'something is up.'

'Yes, it is. It's a secret, but I don't suppose it matters telling you, if you keep it to yourself. Your father's negotiating to take over Topley's furniture business – you know, that little factory over on the other side of Thornleigh. They make kitchen fitments, tables, that sort of thing . . .'

'I thought it was an old family firm.'

'Yes, it is, and has been for donkey's years, but I'm afraid these are changed days, and with inflation and taxation and all the rest of it, they're beginning to feel the pinch.'

'You mean, Crayshaws would start making furniture as well as floorings?'

'Something like that.'

'And who's going to raise the money?'

'That's where Mr Stebbings comes in. Fleming Bernsteins are merchant bankers.'

'I see,' I said, not sure how I felt about all this, but hating the soullessness of big business. Somehow the very name of Mr Stebbings personified this soullessness. He would be bald and thin and have a face like an adding machine. I almost decided that I would go to Roger's barbecue after all, but in the end the balance fell in favour of cold salmon.

———

I heard the car arrive as I was changing. Usually in the evening I wear a clean pair of jeans and a fresh shirt but because company was expected I put on a white, loose dress, previously unworn, with a good deal of ethnic embroidery around the neck and a narrow band of the same around the billowing hem. It felt very cool and soft against my skin, almost as though I were wearing nothing. As I left my room, I could hear my parents talking in their room, and imagined Mr Stebbings also occupied in the guest room, perhaps changing one dull suit for another, and a gloomy tie for some tasteful number in beetroot brocade.

I wandered into the sitting-room and was startled when a male form instantly put down the paper and unfolded itself from a corner of the sofa.

'Good evening,' said Mr Stebbings.

As well as being a natural worrier, I am very shy. Meeting a new person in the presence of my parents is bad enough, but being suddenly flung face to face with one when least expected is inclined to leave me speechless. I mightn't have been speechless if Mr Stebbings had lived up to my dour imaginings. But he was not bald and neither did he have a face like an adding machine. He was tall, with thick dark hair, and quite young – scarcely thirty. His face was deeply tanned and he looked as though he spent some time playing tennis and squash. His eyes were very dark. There was something disconcerting in their steady regard, and I realised that he was waiting for me to say something.

'Good evening.' It came out in a sort of pipe.

'You must be Victoria. I'm John Stebbings.'

We shook hands. It seemed very formal. I said, 'I thought you were still upstairs, getting changed.'

'No. I'm downstairs, reading the newspaper.'

I wondered if he were laughing at me. 'Have you got a drink?'

'Not yet.'

'Would you like one?'

'Thank you.'

My father had left some bottles and glasses out on a tray. I said, 'Would you like to help yourself?'

'All right.' He laid down the newspaper and went to do this thing. 'Can I pour something for you?'

I like white wine and my father had opened a bottle and left it in a bucket of ice, so I said that I would like some of that. He poured it and a sherry for himself, brought both the drinks over to where I stood, and handed me my glass. There was another pause.

I said, 'Would it be nice to go out into the garden? It's still warm.' Somehow I felt it would be easier to cope with him out of doors. We could talk about the roses and the hot weather. He said that he would like that very much, so we went out on to the terrace and settled ourselves in two of the ramshackle chairs which my mother is always promising to replace, and the one that he chose creaked horribly and I prayed that it would not give way beneath that solid weight of bone and muscle.

It didn't.

He said, 'Your father tells me you're going to university in October. What are you going to read?'

'English and History.'

'Have you been away from home before?'

'No, I was at day school.'

'You'll miss all this.' He glanced about him, and I was pleased with his perception, because I knew I was going to miss it badly – the drowsy garden, and the gentle old house.

'Yes, I know I will.' I added, 'It was a vicarage, the house I mean. That's why there are so many bedrooms, to accommodate the enormous families of the Victorian clergy.'

'I don't know whether it's due to the clergy or the children, but it has a charming atmosphere.'

I had begun to feel less shy. I said 'Where do you live?'

'In London. Where I work.'

'Did you always live there?'

'No, I hail from the black North.'

He didn't sound as though he had liked it much. I said,

'My Aunt Charlotte lives in Scotland. In Sutherland. She loves it.'

'It's scarcely the same thing.' His voice was cool, and I wondered if he meant to sound as cutting as he did. To show him that I was not to be intimidated, I asked boldly, 'Is my father's firm going to take over Topley's?' and was rewarded by his expression of astonished disapproval.

'How did you know about that?'

'My father told my mother and my mother told me. Don't worry, I shan't breathe a word. I just wanted to know if it was true.'

'You'll know when it's a *fait accompli* and not a moment before.'

'Does Mr Topley mind being taken over?'

He sent me a glance in which irritation and amusement were mixed in about equal proportions. 'How you do worry a bone! No, I don't think he does. In a way I think he's relieved.'

'Does it mean a lot of people will be made redundant?'

'Perhaps a few. But that's better than the business being declared bankrupt and closing down and everybody losing their jobs.'

I said, 'I hate it.'

'What do you hate?'

'Big business. Big fish swallowing little fish. People losing sight of the only thing that matters, which is other people.'

'You have,' said John Stebbings, 'to trim your craft to the prevailing wind.'

'I like things to stay the same.'

'So do we all. But they don't.' He raised his glass to me. '*Salud*, Victoria,' he said, and even I was not stupid enough to realise that he had purposely closed the conversation.

When dinner was over my father took John Stebbings into his study; the sound of their muted voices came steadily from beyond the panels of the firmly-closed door. After a time my mother took herself off to bed, asking me to make her excuses to our visitor.

I put some soothing Brahms on to the record player and lay on the sofa with *The Mill on the Floss*. I had read it long ago at school, and was now ploughing through it again, and enjoying it a great deal more the second time around. When I am truly into a book, I become unaware of anything else. I only knew that suddenly it had become too dark to read, that the record had finished long ago, that a door had opened and shut, and . . .

John Stebbings materialised out of the gloom and sat himself down at the other end of the sofa, gently moving my feet to one side.

I gazed at him owlishly, slowly remembering who he was. He said, 'You'll strain your eyes, trying to read in this light.'

'I hadn't realised it had got so dark. My mother said to say goodnight to you. She's gone to bed.'

'And your father is telephoning. He told me to come and talk to you.'

Caught in the velvety half-light, we looked at each other.

I said, 'I'm not very good at talking. I mean, I'm not very good at making conversation.'

'Then we'll do something else.'

He was far too close to me. My heart leaped in a panic. For an idiotic instant I imagined being grabbed by him and kissed. Roger had once done this, squashing his lips, unasked, on to my mouth, scratching my face with his moustache. That was why I disliked him.

But this was Mr Stebbings, of Fleming Bernsteins. Desperately, I cast about for some way to entertain him, but only one suggestion came to mind.

'We could go swimming.'

'*Swimming*?' I could scarcely have astonished him more.

'Yes. It's lovely. In the river. There's a pool, and it's very clean and not polluted at all, and quite deep. You can borrow a pair of my father's trunks.'

Suddenly it did not seem quite such an outrageous idea after all. I jumped off the sofa. When he didn't move, I frowned down at him.

'You don't want to?'

'I didn't say that.'

'You're scared!'

'What of?'

'Being cold. Getting wet. Drowning.'

He began to laugh. He put out a hand and I pulled him to his feet. He said, 'What are we waiting for?'

In my room, I found my still-damp bikini and wriggled into it, slipped my feet into an ancient pair of sandals, found my towelling wrap and ran downstairs again. By now it was nearly dark, but there were stars in the sky and a chill dampness in the air. I could feel dew on the grass. I shivered, not from cold, but with a sort of excitement. There has always been something special about the garden at night, as though magic might happen, like in *A Midsummer Night's Dream*. When he came I led the way down the sloping lawn towards the sound of the river.

Beneath the trees he said, 'I can't see a blessed thing.'

'Just a few more feet. There's no mud. Just stones. A sort of little beach.' I dropped my coat and put a foot into the running stream and it felt so cold I let out a yelp.

'Have you changed your mind?'

'No, of course not, it just that . . .'

But he, proving himself much braver than I, had already walked past me, wading into the water and then disappearing with scarcely a splash.

'Come on.' He swam a few strokes, his feet kicking up a small wake. 'Come on, you coward, it was your idea.'

I screwed up my face and courage and followed him. The cold took my breath away, like swallowing knives. When I came up, gasping for air, the darkness seemed total. I looked up, and glimpsed one or two stars twinkling through the branches of the trees. I trod water, trying to get my bearings.

Out of the darkness his voice said, 'Where are you?'

'Here.'

There was a soft sound, a ripple, a movement of water. I

kicked my feet and swam towards the sound, and the next moment my hand rested on a bare shoulder. It felt very smooth and hard and pleasant. He said my name, and it was as though the strong movement of running water had washed us together. His arms were around me, his mouth on my mouth. And now, for the first time in my life, I wanted to be kissed. I wanted the hardness of his cheek against mine.

I managed to say at last, 'I didn't mean this to happen.'

'No,' he said gently, 'I know you didn't.'

I was assailed by a sensation of weightlessness. He, so much taller than I, was well within his depth, and I realised he was wading with me to the bank. I tentatively laid my head on his shoulder and my long hair dripped like a wet rope down his back. We came out of the water, out of the shelter of the trees, and I looked up and saw that the sky, once more, was full of stars.

I had been surrounded by love all my life, the love my parents had for each other, the love they had for me. I had read of passionate love in books, in *Romeo and Juliet*, in *Wuthering Heights*. I had watched it in the theatre, on television, had seen how it happened to people I knew, but had never imagined it happening to me. But now it had happened. I would never be the same. Nothing would ever be quite the same again.

—◦—

The next afternoon John returned to London. I did not mind, because I knew that he would come back. He would write to me, he would ring me up. I went downstairs early each morning to scan the post. Nothing. Each time the telephone rang, instead of loitering in the garden, I went to answer it, disciplining myself not to run. Nothing. I waited for my father to tell me that he was coming back for another visit. But a week passed. Nothing. Another week. Nothing.

I did all the classic things. Played the piano until my back and my fingers ached. Went for exhausting walks, read books. I even lost my never-very-robust appetite.

My parents began watching me in a way that drove me mad, their expressions concerned, their eyes sympathetic. Finally, one day, it began to rain. Rain fell in sheets, unrelenting. I stood at my bedroom window and watched it fall. My tears matched the rain. I could not stop them falling. It was over almost before it had begun. He was never coming back.

My mother, by some marvellous maternal instinct, came to my room and found me face down on my bed and howling. She sat beside me and I turned and hugged her as I had not done since I was a very small child and having nightmares about monkeys.

'It's about John Stebbings, isn't it?' she said at last, when I had cried myself dry and was sufficiently coherent to talk about it.

'Yes.'

'Oh, my darling.' She sounded despairing. 'I was afraid of it. I've been afraid of it ever since he was here.'

I blew my nose. 'Why so afraid?'

'Because he's the sort of person that he is.'

I said as calmly as I could, 'Which is?'

My mother told me. John Stebbings was ambitious. He had shaken off his background in Yorkshire. He had made, through nerve and a certain shrewd ruthlessness, a lot of money. He was not married, but it was well-known in the City that he had a girlfriend as single-minded as himself, and everybody who knew them agreed that they made a good pair. 'She has a chain of dress shops, I think–'

I imagined the woman, cool and slender as a blade of grass, always immaculate. She would never be stuck for conversation. She would never be made speechless by shyness. I supposed that they were living together.

I said, 'Do you suppose he loves her?'

'How can one say? Love comes in so many different shapes and forms. Everybody needs something different.'

I said, 'I thought—'

'No,' said my mother. 'He's not the sort of person you need. You need someone who will put you first, who will take care of you. The person who comes first in the life of a man like John Stebbings is John Stebbings.' And then she said, 'You'll forget him in time, Victoria, believe me.'

———·•·———

It was September. There was crispness in the air, the beginnings of autumn, blackberries on the brambles, the first falling yellow leaves. My mother was due to go on her Scottish holiday.

'I won't go if you don't want me to,' she told me, but I told her not to talk rubbish, that I was perfectly all right, and that I would look after my father. When the time came my father drove her to the airport to catch the plane to Inverness.

Three days later, it happened. It was a Sunday. Rosa had gone off for the weekend and I was in the kitchen, starting to cook Sunday lunch for my father and myself. When the telephone rang, I heard him answer the call from his study. I had no premonition, nothing. When he came into the kitchen, I was occupied at the cooker. I said, 'Do you want white sauce with your cauliflower?'

He did not reply. I turned to look at him and saw him standing in the doorway, his usually ruddy face drained of colour. Fear dropped like a dead weight into the pit of my stomach. He said, 'There's been an accident.'

She had borrowed her sister's car to go to early Service. On the way home, she was involved in a collision with a van which had skidded, out of control, on a dangerous bend. The driver of the van had suffered no more than a few bruises, but my mother had been taken to hospital.

I said, 'But she's going to be all right . . .' Any alternative was unthinkable.

'Yes,' said my father, tonelessly. 'Yes, of course.'

Sunday lunch was forgotten. We could neither of us have eaten it anyway. I packed an overnight bag for my father while he rang the airport.

As he got into the car, he said, 'You'll be all right?'

'Of course. Rosa comes back this evening.'

'I'll ring you as soon as I've seen her.'

I had never felt so alone in my life. I could have gone to Roger's mother, and she would have welcomed me with open arms and been endlessly kind. But I couldn't leave the house, the telephone. I turned off the cooker, put the uneaten Sunday lunch on to dishes in the larder and left it to congeal. I went into the garden and pulled up weeds.

Late that afternoon my father telephoned from the hospital. My mother was unconscious.

———•◦•———

The dreadful day had become a vacuum, a nightmare. It was nearly five o'clock and I had not eaten since breakfast. I made myself a clumsy sandwich, drank a glass of milk. I went into the sitting-room and turned on the television and then turned it off again. I caught sight of my reflection in the mirror, my face like a ghost, my eyes, by some trick of light, transformed into two holes in my face. I went upstairs, and without knowing what I was doing, put on my bikini and went out into the damp grey afternoon, and down the garden towards the river.

The cold deep water received me without a murmur. Above me, the trees dripped and the sky was lowering and grey. There was no warmth, but there was some strange comfort in the flow of the river. I swam for quite a time, deliberately exhausting myself. Somewhere a blackbird sang. Somewhere, somebody called my name.

At first I thought I had imagined it. There was nobody on this still, sad Sunday afternoon who could possibly have called me. And then it came again, unmistakable, robust, a masculine yell of 'Victoria!'

I saw him coming down the garden and it wasn't Roger, the last person I wanted to see. By now I was back on the rock in the middle of our swimming pool. I curled my fingers into the hand-hold and lay against it, waiting and silent.

'Victoria!'

I saw him coming down the garden and it wasn't Roger, it was John Stebbings. I realised, in some surprise, that I had not thought of him all afternoon. Perhaps it was a dream. Perhaps the whole day had been a dreadful nightmare. Perhaps my mother wasn't lying in hospital, my father hadn't gone to be with her, none of it had really happened and in a moment I would wake up.

He had reached the edge of the water. 'Victoria.'

It wasn't a dream. I was too cold for it to be a dream. He was there, only a few feet away, wearing jeans and a polo-necked sweater that was already beaded with damp. He looked different.

'I've been looking for you everywhere. Didn't you hear me call?'

I shook my head. My teeth were chattering.

He said, 'Come out. Now.'

I could feel my heart pumping. I remembered everything my mother had told me about him.

He said, 'If you don't come out now. I shall come in and get you.'

I knew that he would. I let go of the rock and swam across

to where he waited for me. He came to help me, wrapping me instantly in my towelling coat.

'You lunatic. What induced you to swim on a day like this?' He picked up one of the dangling sleeves and dried my face with it, and made one or two dabs at my hair as though he were trying to dry a wet dog.

I said, through chattering teeth, 'There wasn't anything else to do.'

He hurried me back to the house, and sent me upstairs to have a hot bath. I lay in the steaming water as long as I dared, and then emerged to dress in warm trousers and the thickest jersey I owned. While I did this, I could hear him moving about downstairs and when I joined him I found the sitting-room bright with firelight, and that he had found his way around the kitchen and made a pot of tea.

He said, 'Are you warm now?'

I nodded. He poured the tea and handed me a mug. 'Get this inside you.'

I took it, closing my fingers about its warmth. I said, 'I don't know what you're doing here.'

He told me. It seemed that my father had had an appointment with him in the City the following morning. Somehow Father had found the time to ring John at his flat, to tell him that he would be unable to keep it. He had then told John the reason.

'I asked about you,' said John, 'and he told me you were on your own. So I came down to be with you.'

I said, 'Rosa's coming back tonight.'

'Is your mother going to be all right?'

'We don't know. My father's going to ring me when he knows more.'

'Have you had anything to eat?'

'I had a sandwich.' I looked at him again, trying to make myself believe that he was here, he was really here. He had come from London, on a Sunday, in order to be with me, when what I needed more than anything else in the world was the company of another human being.

I said, 'I didn't think I'd see you again.'

'I didn't exactly expect it, either.' His eyes, those dark, bold eyes, went suddenly tender. 'Would you rather I hadn't come?'

The horror of the day had destroyed all my inhibitions. 'It's just that I'm not very good at being hurt like that. It never happened to me before.'

After a little, he said, 'You may not believe this, but I didn't mean to hurt you. You're so young, and . . . innocent, I suppose. And it was a completely new experience for me, and you must believe I was just as shattered as you.'

'You've got a girlfriend in London. My mother told me. After that, I understood.'

'No, you didn't. It's finished.'

'Why?'

'You. You being alone. Your father's phone call came just as we were going out. I said I couldn't go because I was coming here. She was livid. It's not the first time we've been disenchanted with each other. And suddenly I found I was taking a long, cool look at myself. It seemed to me that perhaps for the first time for a long time, I was doing something that was completely right, and honest, and wasn't centred on myself. I'm afraid that sounds faintly self-righteous and sanctimonious.'

'What did your friend do?'

'She easily found a substitute for me, and I came here.'

'I've spoiled it all for you.'

'You spoiled nothing. You opened my eyes.'

'Just because you're sorry for me.'

'There's more to it than that.'

I hadn't drunk any of the tea he had made me. Now I laid down the mug, carefully, as though it were important not to spill a drop. I said, 'I don't want to be hurt again.'

'I won't hurt you ever again.'

———◦—◦◦—◦———

The telephone rang. The double peal slashed across the silence of the house, loaded with foreboding.

We looked at each other. I said, 'That'll be my father,' but I couldn't move.

'Do you want me to answer it?'

I nodded. He went into the study and I stayed by the fire, kneeling on the hearthrug, and feeling the warmth of the flames on my face. I closed my eyes and prayed. I heard his voice through the door, low, firm, giving nothing away. After a minute he came back into the room. I still couldn't move. My mother was going to die.

He pulled me to my feet, saying, 'It's all right. It's not as bad as they feared. She's conscious now and she's going to be all right. Your father was slightly surprised when I answered the phone, but I think quite relieved to know that you weren't alone. He's asked me to stay till he gets back. He says Rosa can chaperone us . . .'

I had stopped listening. I was in his arms again, howling like a baby all over the front of his sweater. Partly because of my mother, partly because I had been so miserable, but mostly, although I had no idea of what was to become of us, because he had come back to me.

Through the Eyes of Love

At Christmastime we all see things differently, for there is magic in the air and anything can happen . . .

There was, Julia Prescott decided, only the finest razor-edge between depression and despair. Depression had been constant for weeks, familiar, creeping up on her like a prowler in tennis shoes. But despair was the dreaded spectre behind the closed door, springing forth just when you least expected it.

This happened on a dark Tuesday afternoon two weeks before Christmas. One moment she was typing busily; the next in a flood of tears. She sat there, and her typewriter and the letter she had been working on melted into a blurred pool of misery.

She might have pulled herself together, wiped her eyes, and blown her nose before anyone could have been the wiser. But just then footsteps came hurrying up the hall, and Dennis Erdmann himself burst through the door.

He stopped halfway across the room.

'My darling girl, what's the matter?'

'Nothing. Everything. I . . .'

'Julia.' Somehow he was at her side, gathering her into a kindly embrace, pressing her face against his monogrammed shirt, stifling her grief in the soft luxury of silk and the scent of King's Gold.

After a little while, Julia felt better. Later still, she was strong enough to draw away from him.

'What's happened?' he asked.

She looked up at him with swollen eyes. 'Just a sort of build-up.'

'I've been working you too hard.'

'It's not that.'

'Then it's Phillip.'

Julia started to deny this but she stopped and gazed at him. She saw the ageless face, boyish despite the soft halo of greying hair. She thought of the millions of women who owned jeans with his name emblazoned across the seat, who slept beneath his flowery sheets or drenched themselves in his exclusive scents – Queenie for women, King's Gold for men.

'Yes, I suppose it is Phillip.'

'Tell me.'

'It's just that he went to New York a month ago on business and that's it. No letters, no phone calls.'

It made her feel marginally better just to talk about it. Perhaps because it was to Dennis she confided. Dennis, who was such a comforting mixture of sympathy and hard-headed good sense.

'He must be out of his mind. But then, he was never good enough for you. Someday you'll be thankful you're rid of him.' He gave her a brisk shake. 'Think about cheerful things. Christmas, for instance.'

'I'd like to sleep and wake up and find Christmas all over with.'

'You don't mean that.' He was visited by a brilliant idea.

'I know, put the cover on your typewriter, put on your coat, and go out and buy lots of lovely presents. That'll cheer you up.'

'I've bought my presents. All of them, except my mother's.'

'Well, go buy something for her. Something marvellously expensive and impractical. What's it going to be?'

Despite everything, Julia found herself beginning to smile. 'I had thought,' she told him, 'about bath towels.'

———

Minutes later she was on her way, heading towards the biggest department store in London. The afternoon was slipping into darkness. It was cold and wet, the streets choked with pre-Christmas traffic. Every shop window was a blaze of light, a marvel of arrangement, a seduction to one's bank balance. All in all, a luscious display of materialism. What had happened to Christmas?

She thought of Phillip, in New York, making his way down the crowded sidewalks, just as she was making her way through London. An ocean between them. But it was not only the ocean that separated them after more than two years together. It was Phillip's ambitions; his fears of being caught, pinned down in domesticity. It was Julia's need for permanence, for a home life as secure as her own had been. She needed this, and Phillip didn't. It was as simple as that.

These chilling reflections had brought her to her destination and she went through the revolving doors into a world of warmth and light and enchanted fantasy.

Her purchase took no time at all. Her mother liked her towels to be plain and white, and Julia was determined they should be fluffy and large. While the package was being wrapped Julia took her wallet out of her handbag and stood at the counter, waiting to pay.

She looked about her. Behind the shelves of stacked linen the walls were lined with mirrors. Her own reflection gazed back at her from between piles of rainbow-coloured towels, and beyond this – slightly out of focus – moved the shifting hordes of other shoppers. A woman in a fur coat, her hair red as a flame, stopped to admire a display of sheets. Then a man moved into view, tall, dark coated. He halted, hesitated, and then began to walk towards the counter where Julia stood. She saw the dark, glossy hair, the very dark eyes, the broad shoulders of a man accustomed to athletic activity. When he was only a couple of paces behind her, Julia turned to face him.

He grinned. 'Julia. I thought it was you.'

She said, 'Hello, Harry.'

For some reason he was the last person she wanted to meet on this bleak afternoon. Harry Bradford. A man who, in some inexplicable way, had been lurking for some time at the end of her life. She was always running into him at unexpected places at unexpected times. She had met him soon after she'd started dating Phillip and had found herself sitting across the table from him at a supper party one evening. Phillip and Harry had gone to school together, but that seemed to be all they had in common. Phillip, for some reason, didn't like Harry. He called Harry a cheerful bore.

'What does he do?' Julia asked as Phillip drove her home from the party.

'He works for an uncle, I think. He's a stockbroker.'

That was the extent of Julia's interest in the man but, like a persistent burr, Harry Bradford's presence was not so easily shaken from her life. She went to a reception with Dennis – to welcome some French fashion promoters – and met Harry Bradford again. Another time, during a summer weekend with friends in Sussex, he turned up at a village fair. And more recently, when she and Phillip had gone to their favourite restaurant for dinner, Harry Bradford and a lovely brunette were seated at a nearby table.

And now here he was again. 'You shouldn't be so tall,' he was saying. 'It makes it impossible for you to melt into a crowd. What are you doing?'

'Christmas shopping.'

'Ask an obvious question, get an obvious answer.' He held up a small package. 'I, too, have been Christmas shopping.'

They both smiled, as though this were particularly amusing. Then he said, 'How are you?'

'Well. Very busy.'

'Still working with Dennis Erdmann.'

'Yes.'

'And how's Phillip?'

It was gratifying to be able to reply, coolly, casually. 'He's fine. He's in New York at the moment, so I haven't seen him for a while. Excuse me . . .'

She turned to receive her package and paid for it with her

credit card. This took a few moments, but at the end of it all, Harry Bradford was still there.

⎯•⎯

They began to walk, slowly, down the thick red carpet of the centre aisle. She wondered if she could lose him by pleading other errands, but when he said, 'I have my car. Can I give you a lift?' the prospect of not having to find a taxi or wait for a bus overcame all reservations. She accepted instantly.

Minutes later she sat beside him in his car with her package on her knees. Now it was dark, and pouring rain. The traffic out of the city was a solid stream, moving with agonising slowness. If it had been Phillip at the wheel there would have been curses and much horn honking, but Harry Bradford seemed totally unaffected by the situation.

'Don't you ever get impatient?' Julia asked, breaking the silence.

'Yes, often. But it doesn't do any good. The traffic's bound to be a nightmare this time of year.' And then, 'Will Phillip be back for Christmas?'

'I don't think so. He'll probably be back after the New Year.'

They moved another few yards and then stopped again.

'What are you going to do for Christmas?'

'Go home.'

'Where's home?'

'Gloucestershire.'

He said, 'I'm going to Gloucestershire for Christmas too. I

usually try to be with my parents, but they've gone to the West Indies this year. My aunt and uncle asked me to spend the holidays with them. They just bought a house in a village called Sudsbury.'

Julia closed her eyes. It can't be true, she told herself.

'Do you know it?'

She opened her eyes. 'Yes,' she said. 'I live there.'

'My aunt bought a house called the Grange.'

'In that case, she's Mrs Carrington.'

'You know her?' He looked pleased. 'What a coincidence.'

They were halted once more at the traffic lights. 'Do you have any brothers and sisters?' he asked.

'Yes, four. Two of each. Two married and with families, two not. And every year we all congregate at Sudsbury, and the old house bulges at the seams. We eat too much and everybody gives everybody else far too many presents.'

'It sounds like fun.'

She said, 'I don't know why one expects so much at Christmas. We aren't children any more. It can't go on being magic.'

'Isn't it magic for you?'

'Not this year.'

They fell silent. When he drew up at her front door, she asked him, out of politeness, to come in for a drink and was thankful when he declined.

'Well . . . thank you for the ride.'

'Maybe I'll see you at Christmas.'

'Maybe.'

Her own front door, her own latch key. She let herself in and heard him start up his engine and drive away. She felt wrung out with every sort of exhaustion. Her mail held some Christmas cards, an invitation, but no letter from New York. Maybe tomorrow, she told herself, as she had been telling herself ever since Phillip left. Maybe tomorrow.

———✦———

She went home the day before Christmas. The train was hot and crowded, but her brother Peter was on the platform waiting to meet her. They hugged tightly, and then he piled her luggage into the old station wagon and bundled her in out of the rain as well.

Julia pulled off her hat. 'Who's home?'

'Everybody. Minnie and I and the children got here yesterday. Rachel caught a bus from Oxford and John hitchhiked from Durham.' That took care of the immediate family. Only Julia's sister Marion and her Naval husband were missing, stationed in Hong Kong for two years.

'And Alan?'

Alan was Marion's only child, a pale, shy little boy of eight, who had always secretly been a favourite of Julia's.

'He's home. He was supposed to fly to Hong Kong, but he's had the flu, and Ma decided it might be better if he didn't make the trip.' He glanced at his sister. 'And how are you? You look pretty weary.'

'I'm fine.' She looked away from him, out into the dark countryside. 'It's good to be home,' she said.

Another fifteen minutes and they were there, Peter blowing a fanfare on the horn, so that by the time they stopped in front of the door all the family came flooding out to meet her.

———•◦•———

Later, leaving Minnie and Rachel to get supper, Mrs Prescott went upstairs to Julia's room, ostensibly to help her unpack, but really to have a private little talk.

'Not that there's much to talk about, but with this crowd I don't know when I'll have another chance to get you alone.'

'You mustn't do too much,' Julia told her. She took a dress from her suitcase and Mrs Prescott was instantly diverted.

'What a lovely dress. Is it a Dennis Erdmann?'

'Yes. Worn by a model so I got it at a discount.'

'You can wear it Christmas evening. I haven't had a chance to tell you, but we're having guests. You remember the Carringtons, don't you? They bought the Grange. They've got some nephew staying with them this year, and I invited them all for cocktails Christmas night.'

'I know the nephew,' Julia said, sounding fatalistic. 'Harry Bradford.'

Mrs Prescott's face took on an expression of alert interest. Julia hastily explained. 'I don't know him very well. I just meet him now and then.' She steered the conversation into a different direction. 'I haven't seen Alan yet. Where is he?'

'Probably in his room.' She got off the bed, tiredly, as though she had been on her feet all day. 'I'll tell him to come and see you. Have a bath if you want. There's a tankful of hot water.'

Julia was brushing her hair when she heard the creak of the opening door. Through the mirror she watched its progress. A pale head appeared around the edge of the door.

'Alan.' She turned to greet him. 'I've been waiting to see you.'

He shut the door carefully behind him. 'I was going to Hong Kong, but I got the flu.' He moved to sit on the edge of the bed. 'I really wanted to go.'

'I know.' She was sympathetic. 'Anyway it's fun for us to have you here. Have you got your presents for everybody?'

'Yes. Daddy sent me some money, and I spent it all.' He hesitated. 'I got you something. I hope you like it.'

'I'm sure I'll love it.'

From downstairs Minnie called his name. 'I have to go and eat supper now.' He grinned. 'I'm glad you're here.

———————

Christmas Eve, Julia and her mother let themselves out of the house and walked the short distance to church. It was a perfect night, starlit and frosty. Her mother took Julia's arm. 'I'm glad it's only us,' she said. The rest of the family planned to go to morning service the following day.

Julia did not reply. In companionable silence, they made their way down the street. Inside the old church was a scattering of people. They found two seats in an empty pew. It was very cold. At the foot of the nave stood a Christmas tree, twinkling with coloured lights. Julia looked at it and remembered other Christmases. The long-ago ones before her father had died, and the Christmases since. Each one a celebration, created by her mother, who had put grief and loneliness aside in order to ensure both magic and memory for her children and grand-children.

Perhaps that was what it was all about. Like being given a present of time. A breathing space to stop brooding on one's own personal woes – to stand away from them.

From the open door behind them came whispered voices, and then the Carringtons appeared, making their way to a forward pew. Harry Bradford was behind them.

Julia realised, with some surprise, that she wasn't put out by his sudden appearance. He was, whether she liked it or not, part of this particular Christmas.

⸻

And then Christmas Day. The usual muddled six-o'clock-in-the-morning mayhem; breakfast in the kitchen, the air rent with cries of excited children. The fire blazed, and beneath the tree presents were piled high.

Julia sat on the floor. Paper and more paper. A book she wanted, a new sweater, a garlic press.

There came a small pause in the happy turmoil. Julia real-ised that Alan stood beside her.

'Thank you so much,' he said, 'for the shirt and for my action man.'

She gave him a kiss. 'I'm glad you like it.'

'This . . .' It was almost a whisper. 'This is your present. From me.'

'Oh Alan.' It was small, shaped like a Christmas card, and it rattled. 'What can it be?' He watched her open it, eyes glittering. The paper fell away. There was a card and cellophane, and between the two a long string of very small, artificial pearls.

'It's beautiful.' She slit the cellophane with her thumbnail and drew the necklace out. String showed between the beads and there was a fastening of tin set with a dubious chip of blue glass.

She put it on. 'How does it look?'

He beamed. 'Will you wear it all day?'

'Yes, all day. And thank you.'

Julia bathed and dressed for the evening. Her dress was coral-coloured with beaded embroidery at the simple neckline and around the cuffs. She fastened Alan's pearls around her neck and tried to imagine Dennis Erdmann's reaction to such sacrilege and found herself laughing. What did it matter? It was Christmas. She only prayed that the flimsy cotton on which the beads were threaded would last the evening, and that Alan would continue to believe he'd given her the best present of the day.

When she went downstairs Peter was arranging a tray of glasses. Someone else brought a bucket of ice, and one by one they all gathered. The doorbell rang at exactly seven o'clock.

After the greetings Harry Bradford made his way straight to Julia's side.

'So we meet after all,' he said, giving her a kiss on the cheek. 'Have you had a good Christmas?'

'Yes marvellous.'

'Are all these children your nieces and nephews?'

'Yes. And this is Alan.'

'Hello Alan.'

They shook hands. Alan was overcome with shyness and Julia helped him out. 'Alan's parents are in Hong Kong, so he's spending Christmas with us. He gave me this.'

She touched the necklace and looked into Harry's face. She expected amusement, the twitch of an eyebrow, a hastily suppressed smile. But he only said, 'Did he? What a splendid present.'

The words were scarcely out of his mouth when the very thing that Julia had dreaded, happened. The flimsy strand of cotton silently parted and dozens of tiny beads poured from the string, down the front of her dress, across the carpet, under chairs, everywhere. There was an appalled silence, and then Alan burst into tears.

Julia went down on her knees and gathered him into her arms. 'Darling, don't cry.'

'I wanted them to last forever,' he wailed into her neck. 'And they didn't even last for a day.'

'It's all right . . . look . . .' That was Harry, also on his knees, already picking up the beads. 'If everybody helps, we can collect them all. They can be restrung.'

They all joined in, treating it as a sort of game. A paper bag was produced to hold the beads, and when no more could be found. Harry folded the bag and carefully placed it on the mantel.

Alan smiled at last. Julia turned to Harry to thank him, but before she could speak, he said, 'I think your phone's ringing.'

It was too. Julia excused herself and went to answer it in the study.

'Julia, what on earth are you doing there?'

It was Phillip.

'Where else would I be? It's Christmas.' Her voice was cool.

'But I came back to be with you. I had no idea you'd light out on me like this.'

'Phillip, I didn't light out on you.' Indignation began to warm to anger.

'Well, come back. Now. Tomorrow.'

'No.'

'Julia, for heaven's sake.'

'Phillip, I'm sorry. There's a party on. We have guests. I have to go.'

She hung up, filled with a smouldering rage and a sort of triumph.

I'm finished with you, she said out loud to the telephone. *You've made me miserable, but not any more. You're not worth any girl's heart.*

After a little while, calmer, but still high with colour, she returned to the others. Mr Carrington was showing the children a card trick, and everyone was watching. Only Harry turned his head her way. For a long moment she met and held his gaze. Then she smiled, found herself another glass of wine, and went to join the others.

In the light of all that had happened, Julia didn't think

about the pearls again until the following morning. When she went to look for the little paper bag, it was not there. After some searching she and her mother decided it had been inadvertently thrown away. Alan, playing with his action man, did not mention them, and with one thing and another they were forgotten by everybody.

Julia neither saw nor heard anything of Harry Bradford after Christmas night, and she didn't expect to. She returned to London, telling herself that somewhere, sometime, she would bump into him again. But several weeks later, just as she returned home from work late one evening, her doorbell rang and there he was.

She felt her pulse quicken and an involuntary smile touched her lips. You fool, she told herself.

'Hello, Harry.'

'Happy New Year,' he said.

'Isn't it a bit late to wish Happy New Year?'

'Never too late.'

'Come in, by the fire where it's warmer.'

He entered on a draught of frosty air, his hands deep in the pockets of his overcoat. 'Am I interrupting you?'

'Not at all. Take off your coat. I'll get you a drink.'

He stood with his back to the fire, watching her as she crossed the room to hand him his drink. Unexpectantly, he said, 'Phillip's back.'

'I know.'

'I ran into him this morning. I asked after you, and he grunted some reply and then changed the subject.'

'He was back at Christmas. He called me during the party.'

'I thought it was he. You came back into the room looking like a woman who'd been talking to the man she loves.'

She said carefully. 'I did love Phillip. I loved him very much. But I don't think we ever wanted the same things. I said goodbye to him that night on the phone.'

'So it's over?'

'Yes.'

'I didn't know. It's the only reason I haven't called you before. It's funny, isn't it, how long we've known each other and yet we don't know each other at all?

'I have something for you,' he said.

Julia frowned. He put his hand into his jacket pocket and drew out a long narrow jewel case, with an impressive name stamped upon its lid. She opened it. Inside lay Alan's string of pearls, a silken knot between each bead, and in place of the tin and blue glass clasp was a tiny circlet of diamonds.

He said, 'I was wrong about you. I always thought you were rather chillingly glamorous and sophisticated, but at Christmas I realised you weren't like that at all. Instead, you're the sort of person who wears artificial pearls with a Dennis Erdmann creation – and gets away with it – just to make a little boy happy. When the party was over I stole the beads. I had them rethreaded and added the clasp as a present from me. I didn't know when I would give them to you. I only knew that, if necessary, I was prepared to wait forever for you.'

'I'm glad it didn't have to be forever.'

'I am too.'

She went to stand beside him, at the fireplace. She put on the necklace, fastening the clasp at the back of her neck, and then she turned to him for admiration. He kissed her. He said, 'If Phillip ended at Christmas, perhaps this New Year is meant for beginnings.'

'You mean, like resolutions and fresh starts?'

'Yes,' said Harry, kissing her again. 'And other things.'

Our Holiday

Polly said, 'Have you told Andrew?'

It was half past eleven in the morning and they sat in Muffin's Parlour in the high street, drinking coffee.

'Yes.' Across the table, the steaming cups of coffee, the plate of homemade scones, Kate's eyes met those of her friend. Despite herself, she laughed. 'Too stupid, being so nervous and diffident . . . as though I were about to tell him that I'd taken a lover or was leaving him forever.'

'What did he say?'

'Bucked slightly. I've never sprung something like this on him before. It was the last thing he was expecting.'

'For heaven's sake, you're only going on a holiday together. I think he should be delighted.'

'It's just that I've never *planned* the holidays before. It's always been Andrew. That's why we always ended up some-where where there was a golf course. And a bit of beach around, of course, when we still had the children to think about. But this time I don't think there is a golf course.'

'Well, I suppose if he was really determined, he could find one.'

'Only the Mediterranean sunshine, red rocks, blue seas, and total relaxation. And lovely food,' Kate added. She had spent hours brooding secretly over brochures. 'And our own huge balcony, and a view of the sea. And there's a swimming pool as well, and tennis courts.

'I didn't know you played tennis.'

'We used to, years ago. And you can put tennis rackets in a suitcase, not like golf clubs which fall off airport trolleys or else get lost and have to be retrieved from a terrible sort of kennel where they put animals and awkward parcels.'

'I know. Like parrots in cages and double basses. Anyway, when Andrew'd stopped bucking, what did he say?'

'He said it would cost a lot of money.'

'That's just the first line of defence.'

'And *I* said I was going to spend old Aunt Dodie's inheritance. And that it was my silver wedding present to him.'

'So what was the second line of defence?'

'There wasn't one, really. He made noises about clipping hedges, and some Diocesan meeting, and then he looked in his diary and turned pages, and finally said "all right".'

'Decent of him.' Polly sounded scathing, but then she was scathing, in a general, openhanded sort of way, about most husbands. Her own had lighted out five years ago, preferring his neat little secretary to his unreliable and disorganised wife, and since his departure, she had had a splendid time, taking up painting and yoga, and working like a beaver to save the environment. When there were motorway demonstrations, Kate was fearful of opening the newspaper in case she caught sight of a photograph of her best friend up some tree.

She drank her coffee. She didn't normally indulge in morning coffee in little cafés, but this morning was different, because it was all so important. She was forty-seven, she had done something totally out of character, and she had to talk about it to somebody. Polly was the only friend she truly trusted to keep her mouth shut. She had telephoned her and made this little date. Muffin's Parlour at eleven. And Polly, scenting a cry for help, had come.

Now she said, 'Kate, there's a reason for all this, isn't there?'

'I told you. A silver wedding. Twenty-five years.'

'But something more.'

There was, of course. Kate said, 'Yes.' Polly waited. 'Perhaps just having time together. Just doing things together. It was like that for a little, and then it all slipped away. The children came, and then business flowered and prospered and took up all Andrew's time. And when he wasn't being a successful lawyer, he was . . . well, you know.'

'Yes, I know. Playing golf, and being chairman of this committee, and that committee, and raising funds for the church steeple, and running the tombola at the Cricket Club fête.'

'I suppose it happens to every couple. You simply drift apart, but with children there isn't time to notice it, because you're so busy looking after *them*. But then the children leave home. Robbie's at university and Emily's started her cooking course, and the house is an empty nest. Cliché, cliché. I feel the need to start again.'

'How's your sex life?'

'However it was, I wouldn't tell you. But I've not yet reached the age when the greatest physical joy is the warmth of the sun on my back.'

'Second honeymoon?'

'No. Not that. Just a chance to stop the rot.'

'Think it'll work?'

'I'm hoping.'

'What if it doesn't? Would that be the end of the world?'

'No. It would just go on being the same.'

The next two weeks were taken up with furious preparation. Kate bought clothes, a sun hat and a pair of white trousers and something called a Cover Up. She bought sun oil and sandals and paperbacks and a new bottle of scent. She bought, feeling an idiot, a new nightdress.

Andrew, as well, made his more prosaic arrangements. He spent some evenings telephoning. Cancelling a fund-raising meeting, a dentist's appointment, a golf match.

'Sorry, old boy, but can't be helped. Get Harry or the Major to partner you. And we'll fix a game the moment I get back.'

This last caused Kate a pang of guilt. Andrew's men friends meant much to him and it made him feel badly to let them down. But she resolutely pretended not to listen. It was, she told herself, only for two weeks. Surely for two weeks he could do without his buddies, Harry and the Major, and Charley Foster, his boozy old schoolfriend. Surely for two weeks, they would find enough to do, to amuse themselves, to talk about. She was a bit anxious about talking because she didn't want them to be one of those couples who munch their way through restaurant dinners without a single word to say to each other.

What would they talk about? She resolved to save up lively topics, like having the dining-room painted, and planting a new rose-bed. And they would go for small outings. She had arranged for a hired car. They would drive into the mountains, inspect castles and olive groves, look for wild flowers, find local tavernas for lunch and a drink.

And read. At home Andrew never read a book, being taken up most evenings with the newspapers and the contents of his bulging briefcase. But perhaps, bereft of these, he would take to books. She would pack the latest Dick Francis, which she had already read, and then Andrew would read it and they could talk about that.

He put down the phone at last, took off his spectacles and asked her if she would like a drink. It was seven o'clock now. He always asked her if she would like a drink at seven o'clock. And she said, as she always did, that she would like a small sherry. When he had disappeared to get this for her, she dropped the evening paper, and gazed, unseeing through the window. Outside the garden was darkening into twilight, and she thought that when they were away, she wouldn't drink sherry, but sparkling, chilled wine. Perhaps champagne. And she saw herself on the verandah of their bedroom, dressed in her new white trousers, doused in her new scent, and sipping champagne. The sky would be filled with stars, and the air scented with some unknown but fragrant shrub. Perhaps there would be music. Dancing . . .

She must remember to stop the papers and the milk. Find someone to feed the cat, book the dog into kennels. Her husband returned to her and handed Kate her sherry. He had poured himself a gin.

She said, 'Thank you, darling,' and he raised his glass and said, 'Good health.'

But Kate said, 'Here's to our holiday.'

———

The journey, her plans, went perfectly. The flight was on time. No hang-ups, no forgotten tickets, passports in order. On the plane they had lunch, and there was a small-sized bottle of Chardonnay for each of them, and even the plastic food tasted new and delicious simply because she hadn't produced it herself.

They touched down at half past three in the afternoon, the plane sliding out of the sky to a little airport where palm trees tossed their heads in the warm breeze, and the surrounding mountains stood, velvety. Even the hired car transaction took place smoothly, and Andrew signed a paper or two, paid a deposit and was given a key. It was a small red Seat, and totally adequate. With luggage stored, they took possession.

Kate said, 'There's even a map.'

Andrew shucked off his jacket, and now rolled up his sleeves.

'I'll drive and you navigate,' he told her.

'Remember we're on the other side of the road.'

'If I forget, someone will doubtless remind me. How far is it to the hotel?'

'No idea. Does it matter?'

'It would be good to arrive before dark.'

'We will.'

They did too. Nothing went wrong. Nobody hooted angrily at them, and the road peacefully wound ahead and led them in the right direction. They passed through a small town where the streets were only wide enough for one car at a time. In the centre of this was a square with a church. Bells tolled and locals sat out on the cobbled pavements and doves circled the air around a fountain. Nobody took much notice of them.

'They're used to tourists,' Andrew observed.

'I hate that word. Tourist.'

'What are we then?'

'Visitors. Adventurers. You fork right here.'

They came to their destination by way of a byroad which headed for the sea. There were umbrella pines and the smell of salt, and then a wide promenade and a huge bay, filled with yachts and other delectable craft. Their hotel, The Splendide, stood in the curve of this bay, approached by a driveway of pink oleanders. The hotel was pink, too, with green shutters, its face smothered with purple bougainvillea. As they drew up, a uniformed porter came down the steps to take care of them.

'Señor. Señora. Welcome. Leave your baggage, I shall see to it. Please. Come in.'

She had been so afraid that she would be disappointed. That there would be some unthought, unimagined flaw about which the travel agent had forgotten to warn her. But The Hotel Splendide was perfect. Large and cool and glamorous and shiningly clean. They were transported upstairs in a golden lift, led along corridors of polished wood. A key was turned in a door, and the door opened to a room dimmed by closed shutters. While Andrew dealt with the porter and the suitcases, Kate, feeling like a woman in a film, crossed the floor and threw back the shutters and stepped out and into a dazzle of light. On the balcony were two cane chairs and a low table, and on the table was a bucket, filled with ice, and a frosty bottle of champagne. She went to lean bare arms on the sunwarmed parapet, and saw below her the garden, ablaze with scent and colour. And the swimming pool, and the oleander trees. Beyond stretched the curve of the bay, still and pearly in the evening light.

———— ·•·• ————

While she unpacked, Andrew lay on his bed, and tried to finish *The Times* crossword which he had started on the plane.

'How's your poetry?'

'Try me.'

'The blank is withered by the lake. Five letters with D in the middle.'

'Sedge. Sedge is withered by the lake.'

'Brilliant.' He filled in the letters. 'How did you know that?'

'It swam up out of my subconscious.'

She had a shower in the bathroom that was white-tiled and liberally supplied with soaps and towels and robes. Then she got dressed again, while Andrew showered. He emerged from the bathroom with a towel around his waist and found her at the dressing table, trying to do something with her hair.

He said, 'Is that a new dress?'

'No, old as the hills.'

'It looks new to me.'

He put on his blazer and his cricket club tie. She would have liked to sit on their balcony in the velvety, starlit dark, and sip champagne, but Andrew opted to go down to the bar. He needed the buzz of company and a large gin and tonic.

The bar was busy, but they found a table, and settled themselves, and Kate was aware of interested glances in their direction. New guests. She felt a bit self-conscious and hoped they passed muster. Then a waiter came, and Andrew ordered wine for Kate and a gin and tonic for himself, and there were nuts and black olives in a little dish and it all began to feel quite festive.

The fact that he had told her she was brilliant, and then admired her dress, all in the space of ten minutes, gave her confidence. She said, 'In the plane, I was reading a guide book of the island. There's a monastery up in the hills, not too far. Perhaps tomorrow we could take the car and go and look for it. Unless, of course, you want to relax. Swim in the pool.'

He did not reply. She looked at him, and realised that he was not listening to her. Instead his attention had been caught by a pretty girl sitting at the bar with her boyfriend. Or maybe her husband. But they didn't *look* married, and she had long tanned legs revealed by the smallest of mini skirts. They were laughing.

She experienced a moment of panic, suddenly terrified that she had bitten off more than she could chew. She heard her own voice, disembodied, as though it had nothing to do with Kate, 'The guide book says that a very famous writer used to live there. With his mistress . . .'

No good. He was gone from her, his head turned, his face turned away. Silenced, Kate gazed at the back of his head. And then it seemed, something or someone caught his eye, and he was instantly alert, almost pricking his ears, reminding her of their dog spying a rabbit, or hearing the front door bell ring.

She made a last, valiant effort, '. . . of course, it's a restaurant now, but it might be worth a visit. It has a marvellous view . . .'

Andrew said, 'Good God,' and his voice rang with astonished delight. He swung around to face her, smacking a triumphant hand on his thigh. 'I simply don't believe it.'

'What don't you believe, Andrew?'

'Old Rodney Cumberwell. Sitting over there, by the window.'

She had never heard of Rodney Cumberwell. 'Who's Rodney Cumberwell?'

'That chap in a white jacket.' She looked and saw the white jacket, the sun-reddened face, the fuzzy hair rough as a tweed. Rodney Cumberwell had a moustache, and was with a lady of large proportions, dressed in a bunchy floral skirt and a white blouse with a frilled collar.

'You know him?'

'Met him last spring. Played against him at Wentworth. And the extraordinary thing was that we'd been at school together, only of course he was younger than me and in another house, so our paths never crossed.' All at once Andrew looked quite different. Dynamic and smiling, a man with an aim in life, a quest. 'You don't mind if I go and have a word, do you, darling? The most extraordinary coincidence.'

She said, 'No. Of course . . .'

He went, walking away from her across the polished floor and helpless, hopeless, she watched him go. A moment, and then old Rodney Cumberwell caught sight of Andrew. His reddened face lit up with joy, he sprang to his feet, and the two men met, laughing and talking, slapping shoulders, exclaiming in loud, embarrassing British voices, what a strange thing to happen, how wonderful to see you old man, what a coincidence.

It does not matter, Kate told herself. Perhaps coming here, alone, wasn't such a good idea after all. It doesn't matter. She finished her wine, and ate a nut, and the waiter came and replenished her glass.

After a little, Andrew returned to her, his face alight with enthusiasm. 'They only arrived three days ago. He's been trying to find a partner for a golf game. Apparently there's a championship course only five miles away. Did you know that?'

'You haven't brought your clubs.'

'No problem. Rodney says we can hire some from the Pro. He's already done a recce. I said we'd have dinner with them, and then we can make a few plans. You don't mind, do you, darling? The most extraordinary thing. Running into Rodney Cumberwell in this neck of the woods.'

'Yes,' said Kate faintly. But Andrew looked happy. Perhaps that was what holidays were all about. To make people look happy. 'Is that his wife?'

Andrew's eyes twinkled. 'Well, she certainly isn't his mistress. Come and be introduced. Be social.'

She wondered if she should stand up and start screaming. *I do not want to be introduced. I do not wish to meet the Cumberwells. I want to swim and look for wild flowers and drink champagne and be with you.*

But, of course, she did not. It was no good. It was too late. She finished her wine and set down the empty glass. She looked across the room, and saw Mrs Cumberwell was smiling at her. Mrs Cumberwell, with her new perm and her swollen feet stuffed into her best court shoes.

Kate got to her feet, and, following her husband, went to be introduced to the unknown lady, in whose company, she knew, she was going to spend the next two weeks.

Harbour of Love

Most nights, from this old house, you could hear Lake Michigan – a distant murmur of endless breakers, rolling up and over the sand. The air smelled of fresh water, and a warm breeze moved the curtains at the open window of Julia's bedroom, where she lay wide-eyed and unsleeping, as the hall clock, deep in the darkness, chimed away the small hours of the morning.

Alone, she thought of Ivan. He was still in London. He had gone for a month on business. A lesser man would have said to Julia, 'Come with me,' but Ivan respected her job as a fashion magazine editor – her devotion to it, her competence. 'I'd give anything to show you London,' he said instead, 'but there'll be other times when we can travel together.'

'That's a promise,' Julia told him, and he had laughed and kissed her, sealing the agreement.

She had not known then that she would not see him again. While he was away, Julia received a phone call from her mother, and her world, her whole secure and satisfying existence was blown sky-high, as totally as if someone had deliberately placed a bomb beneath it.

Barbara and Tony, her sister and brother-in-law, had flown to Colorado for a vacation, a second honeymoon. The plane had crashed in the mountains and there were no survivors. Christopher, their three-year-old son, had been left in northern Michigan with his grandparents, in the warm, comfortable house along the eastern shore of Lake Michigan where Barbara and Julia had grown up.

At first, numb with shock, making a few necessary arrangements, getting into her car to drive the long way from Chicago to her parents' home, Julia had thought of no one but Barbara. But as the shock wore off, and grief swelled to take its place, there was room, too, for other chilling truths. Tony had had no other family, so now, for little Christopher, there were only his grandparents and his Aunt Julia. Words like duty and responsibility filled her mind. Who was to shoulder the responsibility for the little boy?

For the next three weeks Julia thought of little else, and the answer was clear. Of course she must raise Christopher. Julia's parents had had their children late in life. Her mother was now sixty-eight, her father nearly eighty. Christopher was a demanding and active little boy who cried at night because his mother and father had gone and he didn't know where. In the face of such circumstances, every other consideration simply paled into insignificance. Christopher must be cared for and Julia's parents could not be expected to start over again with a small grandchild. It would not be fair to them and it would not be fair to Christopher.

It would be best if Julia and Christopher stayed near her parents but not underfoot. There was a small cottage at the end of the road that led to her parents' house. Old Mrs Martin had lived there for as long as Julia could remember, but several years ago, when she died, Julia's father had bought the cottage, restored it, and had since rented it as a vacation home. Now, at the end of summer, the cottage stood empty, providing Julia with a solution. She would pay rent to her parents to keep things on an even keel for them, and she and Christopher would move in, close to their only family, yet still on their own.

It meant giving up the job she loved, selling the small house she had worked so hard to buy, and leaving all the friends she had made in Chicago. It meant leaving Ivan . . .

———

Now, unable to sleep, Julia remembered meeting Ivan more than a year ago. A young couple had moved into the house across the street from where Julia lived. She had introduced herself to them, welcomed them to the block, and they began a casual, neighbourly friendship. So, a month later, when they threw a housewarming party, Julia was invited.

She had worked hard at the office that day and almost didn't go to the party but finally decided that she must. As she rang their doorbell, she told herself she would stay only five or ten minutes.

There were footsteps down the hall and the door opened. Julia stood there, smiling, expecting one of her new young friends, but instead she saw a very tall, dark-haired man, carrying a small tray of glasses.

He said at once, 'I'm not the butler.'

'Aren't you?'

'No. I'm your host's cousin. The name's Ivan Peele. Come on in.'

Julia entered and he shut the door behind her. 'For some reason, you don't look as though you've come far,' he said.

'From just across the road. I live there.'

'Oh, you're the beautiful neighbour I've been hearing about. Julia, isn't it?'

'Yes it's Julia. But you shouldn't believe all the gossip you hear.'

'You mean about you being beautiful? But they were right. You are.' He handed her a glass. 'Have a drink,' he said, 'and let's go join the party.'

She was twenty-seven and had known many men, but walking through the open doorway in the company of this tall, handsome stranger was like nothing she had experienced before. She felt that she *was* beautiful and exciting. The modest housewarming was, all at once, the most delightful party she had ever been to.

Later, Ivan asked her to have dinner with him. They slipped away from the party and walked around the corner to a little Greek restaurant. Talking to him wasn't like finding out things about a new person, it was like being with someone you had known for years, and as though, at any moment, either of you might say, 'Do you remember . . .'

He told her about his job. Electronics, an international agency, exports . . . Julia heard his words, but she wasn't really listening. She noticed his warm, deep voice, his brown eyes that crinkled at the corners when he smiled. She thought, no man so charming could not be married. And when she learned that he was not married, she was surprised at the happiness that filled her.

They saw each other often after that, spending warm summer evenings in the brightly lit city. By day they took long walks together, or picnicked in the park. Once, they drove out into the country, stopping along the side of a quiet road under a canopy of giant trees to eat the lunch they'd packed. It was, then, for the first time, that Ivan spoke of marriage. Not marriage to Julia, but simply the business of getting married.

'Not yet,' he told her. 'Not for a long time, I think. Does that bother you?'

She thought about it. She said truthfully, 'No. I'm not all that eager to get married myself just now. Three of my friends were married last year and not one of the marriages lasted more than nine months. I think that's a mess.'

'And you're happy, staying the way you are?' he asked.

'So happy that I don't want anything to change it.'

Ivan reached for the wine bottle and emptied the last of the wine into their glasses. 'You know, my love,' he said, 'we're so alike in so many ways. It seems a small miracle.'

She leaned forward to kiss him. 'I like being like you,' she said.

'I like being like you too. The only thing is, I'm not as pretty.'

He disappeared from time to time. His work took him to Europe, Japan, China. Now he was in London, gone for a month. Julia had driven him to O'Hare Airport and seen him off. 'Meet me when I get back,' he told her, and she promised that she would.

———◦•◦———

The next morning, while her father gardened and her mother took Christopher with her into town for groceries, Julia wrote to Ivan. The letter should have been a difficult one, but it was not, because she had always spoken to him as she thought, and now she wrote as though she were speaking to him. She told him everything that had happened, explaining why she must leave Chicago; she wrote:

> *I know I can't come back. I won't be at the airport when you return, but this letter will be waiting at your apartment, so hopefully you won't have too long to wonder what has happened to me.*
>
> *Knowing you and having this year together has been the sort of miracle that doesn't happen to many people. How lucky I am, and how thankful that we didn't make a permanent commitment to each other. The more tenuous the ties that hold us together, the easier it is to say goodbye.*
>
> *My love,*
> *Julia*

The weather, which for days had been mild and damp and overcast, suddenly brightened. It was the middle of September, but the day was as warm as midsummer, and Christopher wanted to go to the beach. Julia led him to their usual picnic spot, a secluded stretch of sand and dunes out of reach of the wind. The lake was a deep blue and there were random sailboats scattered about the curve of the bay.

They walked together to the edge of the lake, and Julia

helped Christopher fill his bucket with sand to build a castle.

'Did you and Mommy do this when you were little?' he asked.

'Oh, yes.'

'That was in the olden days.'

'Yes,' Julia said. 'Things are different now. It's not your mother and me. It's you and me.'

Christopher did not comment on this. He seemed, suddenly, very little, very vulnerable. Julia thought fiercely: I won't let him forget his mother. I won't let him miss out on all the good things Barbara would have wanted for him. It will be so worthwhile. It has to be worthwhile, otherwise there is no point in living a life without Ivan.

The more tenuous the ties that hold us together, the easier it is to say goodbye to you. She had written that a week ago, wanting him to believe that it was true, but the truth was that she felt as though she had been torn up by the roots.

Christopher had been absorbed in his sand castle, but now he looked up, over Julia's shoulder. There had been no sound of footsteps behind her, but suddenly a long shadow moved forward. A man sank down on his haunches beside her, his face level with hers. 'Hello, Julia,' he said.

It was Ivan.

Only her imagination could have brought him to this empty, lonely place. He was in London.

Ivan read her thoughts. 'I had to come back a few days early. Your letter was waiting for me – a real eye-opener of a letter. I drove all night to get here. Someone in town directed me to your folks' house, and your father told me where I could find you.'

He spoke as though it were the most normal procedure in the world, but his casual voice did not convince her. She put her hand on his shoulder and felt the warmth of his body, reassuring herself he was real.

Christopher had not resumed his digging. He knelt there, silent, gazing at the tall stranger. Ivan smiled at him. 'Hi Chris.'

Christopher did not reply, but went back to his digging.

'Julia,' Ivan said softly, 'I think you're crazy.' He said it kindly, so that the words had no sting to them. 'There has to be another alternative, you know.'

'You suggest one,' she said.

'Come back to Chicago.'

'Oh Ivan. It's too late. Where I go, Christopher has to go too. I sold my house. Where would we live?'

'With me,' he answered simply.

It was an astonishing suggestion. 'It can't work,' she said.

'Why not?'

'Well, because of everything. I couldn't just live with you. Not with a child.'

'I wasn't asking you just to live with me. I was asking you to marry me. We could buy a house, big enough for all of us.'

'Oh.' She found herself torn between laughter and tears. 'I'm not as desperate as that. Please don't be sorry for me.'

'Sorry for you? My darling girl, I love you. I simply can't

live without you. It's as simple as that. I need you. I think you need me. And Christopher needs us both.'

'But you were so happy just as you were.'

'It will be different, but just as good. We might even have other children. It happens, you know.'

'And what would you do with a house full of children?'

'What every other man does. Love them, yell at them, bring them up. Until now I have never felt the need to marry. With you, it's become the most important thing in the world to me. Say yes, Julia. Say yes now.'

But before she could say anything, Christopher let out a shout of excitement. Shallow waves slapped at the sandcastle.

Ivan got to his feet. 'Here,' he said, picking up a spade, 'make a channel. The water will run into a moat and save the walls.' The water rushed over his shoes, soaking the bottom of his pants.

Christopher and Ivan worked frantically to save the castle, but Julia stayed where she was, sitting on the sand with her arms wrapped around her knees. Like the unstoppable incoming waves, Julia felt happiness flow through her body. She looked at Ivan with his ruined shoes and his trousers wet to the knees. He did not seem to mind, and indeed, why should he? On such a day, at such a time, this tiny instant out of a whole life, it seemed as though nothing could ever matter again.